IN PARIS–

THE UNCOMMON
DETECTIVES RETURN

IN PARIS–
THE UNCOMMON
DETECTIVES RETURN

MAHIJIT BHATT

ZORBA BOOKS

ZORBA BOOKS

Publishing Services by Zorba Books, November 2019
Website: www.zorbabooks.com
Email: info@zorbabooks.com
Copyright © MAHIJIT BHATT

Cover designed by Dhiraj

Print Book ISBN: 978-81-943110-0-3
eBook ISBN: 978-81-943110-1-0

Zorba Books Pvt. Ltd. (opc)
Sushant Arcade, Next to Courtyard Marriot, Sushant Lok 1,
Gurgaon – 122009, India

Contents

Contents

Prologue

In a prison far from the harbour of Victorian London one night three miserable cats were sulking in a cell.

A ginger tabby with a damaged leg spoke up, 'This place is horrible! The food served here tastes like it has gotten spat on by an elephant! And I will suffocate if I have to do more slave labour in that dirty ground!'

'Be quiet, Flame' said a white tortoiseshell who had a tail tip missing.

'Oh! Shut up Snow, you also hate doing slave labour in a field which has been pooed on by dogs (that was not true he was so fed up of staying in the prison that he was saying such things) I am sure!' said Flame.

'Actually I kind of like doing slave labour as it is the least we can do for the robberies we committed' said Snow.

'What! A disgrace to the cat burglar species who likes being in prison and doing slave labour in a ground which will win the

dirtiest ground in London award every time'
snapped Flame.

'Oh! Yes I have more brains than you, let
me ask you a question, how much is 3 + 3?'
asked Snow.

Flame thought for a minute and answered,
'3 + 3 = 33'.

'Wrong!' said Snow.

'You filthy liar! You know-it-all! You mouse
eyed and rat headed idiot!' exclaimed Flame
and he leaped onto Snow and they rolled off
the wooden bench and started fighting on the
floor.

'Will you two please shut up!!!!!!' shouted
the third cat. He was a brown Persian and he
had very sharp claws that scratched on the
hard walls and very cruel and cunning eyes
and he was not the sort of cat you wished to
meet in a dark alley on a stormy night.

'No way Norbert! This filthy liar and
disgrace to the cat burgling species deserves
to be thrashed!' yelled Flame as he continued
wrestling with Snow.

'That's it' growled Norbert. He leaped
down and separated the two cats and pinned
them against the wall with his paws on their
throats and glaring at them. 'Now listen up

stupid ginger scum and fluffy cloud scum' he started to say.

But Snow cut him off and said, 'We do have names you know'

'Until you prove that you are not stupid, worthless, and useless I will call you stupid ginger scum and fluffy cloud scum' he answered back.

'Will you let go of our necks? We are suffocating,' requested Flame.

'As you wish' answered Norbert and let go so suddenly that they fell onto the floor. 'Now listen up I know how to get out of here' he continued.

'Really?' asked Flame, excited

'Yes, you remember your three friends Night, Leaf and Shorty I am sure?' asked Norbert.

'Our good friends!' answered Snow, also delighted now.

'Yes, them' said Norbert, 'Apparently they have found us an employer who is willing to bust us out and will pay us to steal' he continued.

'How did they send this message to you?' asked Flame.

'Pigeon post and I sent back a message accepting his proposition' answered Norbert.

'So what is our employer like?' asked Snow.

'Night, Leaf and Shorty have never seen him themselves but they know he is nice' answered Norbert.

'When is he coming to bust us out?' asked Flame.

'In three nights but we have some work ourselves to do for this escape' answered Norbert.

'What type of work?' asked Snow.

Norbert held up three spoons (he had sneaked them in from the dining room during supper that evening) and gave one each to Snow and Flame. He then led them over to one loose brick and started scraping off the dust and dirt with the spoon.

'We have to scrape the dirt off so that we can remove the brick and just squeeze through and our employer will take care of the rest' he said.

Snow and Flame also started scraping but after some time Flame stated, 'What I really want is revenge on Nick and Francis!'

'Don't worry stupid ginger scum, revenge shall find its way to us. Now let me tell you the plan' said Norbert. Then he started scraping off the sand and started whispering the plan to his gang.

Chapter 1

A Camouflaging Mission

The next night three dark shapes could be seen jumping across the rooftops of London. The one in the front was a golden spaniel who had mastered the art of jumping from rooftops and even shinning them up like a cat.

How he learnt it was no mystery as just behind a friend was there. A cat. He was a black and white Siamese and had very green eyes and it was he who had taught the spaniel how to jump like a cat.

'We should be getting close to the place for our mission, Nick' he said jumping next to the spaniel.

'Yes you are right, Francis' said Nick 'I am sure the building is very close by where we have to stop a robbery'

'Can I get some help back here, please?' asked the third figure, also another cat but black in colour and a cousin of Francis.

1

'Sure, Simon' answered Francis as he ran behind to help his cousin across the rooftops along with Nick.

'I still can't believe you get to join us as a spy in the Detective and Spy House Agency' said Francis.

'Don't forget it was your cousin who convinced the High Council to open up for cats' said Nick 'and we got promoted to spies after catching Norbert, Flame and Snow and everything stolen was returned to its rightful owners'.

'I wish I could see them eating all that prison food and sulking around and I hope they don't try to escape' said Simon, worriedly.

'Don't worry those three might be smart but they aren't smart enough to escape from such a high security prison' said Francis.

'I think we have reached the place' said Nick stopping and Francis and Simon stopped as well. A big building was in front of them and they could see a window which was reachable and by luck it was open.

They sneaked inside and stepped quietly because they didn't want the people sleeping in there to wake up and find them.

'I am having trouble seeing where I am going' whispered Nick.

'Don't worry, we cats can see in the darkness so we will help you' Francis whispered back.

They crept to the top floor of the building and they could see a jewel box glinting on a table.

'Let's hide, he could be here any minute' whispered Simon as he went and hid behind a chair close by Francis who went and buried himself in an old blanket and lay still.

Nick saw a gap in the floor and crouched there. They had barely settled when there was a noise outside the window and it opened and a pigeon came in with a chameleon riding on its back.

'Look Pidgey! There is the jewellery, let's see what is inside' said the chameleon and the pigeon flew over to the table and gently opened the box and inside a bright golden ring flashed in the moonlight.

'What a beautiful ring!' exclaimed the chameleon. He took it up in his paw and was putting it in a bag (which was attached to the side of the pigeon) when Nick and the cats jumped out of their hiding places.

'Stop Mr. Disguises! We are from the Detective and Spy House Agency and you are under arrest. Now drop the ring and come with us' said Simon.

'So my reputation precedes me' said Mr. Disguises 'I am not giving up the ring nor myself and Pidgey to you'. Saying that he put the ring in the bag and jumped onto the pigeon and commanded it to fly.

The pigeon was just flying up when Francis whispered under his breath 'Oh no you don't' as he took a gun from his bag (he and Nick and Simon were all carrying one with their gadgets in it) and pulled the trigger.

Immediately a laser rectangle caught the pigeon around the wings and brought it crashing onto the floor and Mr. Disguises and the ring fell out.

'Give up now!' ordered Nick.

'Never!' hissed Mr. Disguises and he leaped into the shadows and camouflaged himself.

'What do we do now?' asked Nick and to his surprise Francis went over to the walls and hit a place and Mr. Disguises tumbled out.

'How did you find me?' questioned Mr. Disguises.

'I can smell your filthy skin half a mile away!' answered Francis.

'You can smell me, ah? Well, try this!' said Mr. Disguises as he leaped to his fallen assistant and took out a spray with his tail and pressed it so that it went over Nick, Francis and Simon and made them choke.

'This spray will temporarily disable your sense of smell but give me enough time to get away' said Mr. Disguises as he picked up the ring with his tail and jumped to the window.

He cast his tongue onto a clothes line nearby and swung onto the rooftop of the next building, popped the ring into his mouth and scuttled away.

'Oh no! You won't get away' said Nick and he took out a small bundle of cloth from his bag and pressed a button which turned it into a glider. Then he grabbed hold of it and flew out of the window. Francis and Simon also did the same and flew after him.

Mr. Disguises was humming a tune in his head as he continued to run away onto the street. He felt bad about leaving his assistant behind but small sacrifices had to be made.

'Stop Mr. Disguises!' yelled a voice above him and he saw the spaniel gliding above him followed by the two cats also gliding behind him. His face turned to alarm as the black cat took out a gun from his bag with one paw and started firing paintballs at him.

He started dodging and he climbed up onto a wall as a purple paintball hit right in front of him but he jumped over it and jumped down and disappeared. He came out and camouflaged into the wall as the dog came out of the alley but surprisingly batted a paw at him and flung him out of his disguise and onto the pavement as the ring popped out of his mouth and was picked up by the black cat and he was picked up by the dog.

'Well after we return the ring it's off to jail for you and your assistant' said the dog.

'But how did you find me? It should be an hour before you get your sense of smell back!' asked Mr. Disguises.

'When you jumped over the purple paintball your tail got smeared with purple and it showed when you were camouflaged' answered the dog.

Mr. Disguises looked at his tail and indeed saw some purple on it. He dipped his head in shame as the dog carried him off.

Chapter 2

The Escape

'The night has finally come' thought Norbert, 'The night our employer rescues us and we start out new like phoenix rising from the ashes of despair.'

After three nights and days in the prison they were ready to escape. He had set Flame and Snow to work on some last minute clearing of the dirt of the brick by which they would get out of while he kept an eye out for their employer.

'Is he here yet?' asked Flame for the umpteenth time while scraping off dirt.

'For the umpteenth time stupid ginger scum no! Now you and fluffy cloud scum hurry up and finish! He can come any second' answered Norbert.

Flame sighed and continued scraping off dirt. He wished that he could quit the gang but by himself he wouldn't last a week alone so all this was better than living by himself. Norbert continued looking out of the window for some movement and to his delight he heard a low sound coming from towards the sea. It was getting louder by the second and soon a big machine came flying towards the prison.

It was bright red in colour and had a tail like structure at the end and one wing like structure on either side in the middle and small fans under them and a propeller in the front. He didn't know what it was but whatever it was definitely his employer coming to bust them out of the horrible prison.

'Stupid ginger scum and fluffy cloud scum, our employer is here. Have you completed scraping?' asked Norbert.

'Yes we have' answered Snow.

'Good! Come up here and see his machine, then we escape' said Norbert as Snow and Flame jumped up on the bench and started in astonishment at the machine in front of them which had stopped at the edge of the prison and stood, hovering.

'Beautiful!' exclaimed Flame.

'What a machine!' exclaimed Snow beside them.

'Come on, no dilly dallying, let us put the plan in action' ordered Norbert. He went over to the brick and pulled it open and inside was just enough space for them to crawl through and a small tunnel which would take them out.

'You two go first' ordered Norbert as Snow and Flame crawled through and he was just about to follow them when a shout at the door brought his attention. He turned and saw a prison guard standing with a shocked expression.

Norbert just smirked at him and shot down the tunnel and stood with Snow and Flame at the edge and looked over the prison courtyard and beyond that the sea.

'Now let us jump towards the sea' said Norbert.

'What! We don't know how to swim!' exclaimed Snow and Flame together.

'That was the plan so hurry' ordered Norbert as he took a flying leap while shouting, 'GERONIMO!'

'Guess we have no choice' whimpered Snow.

'Goodbye cruel world' sniffed Flame as they both held each other's arms, closed their eyes and jumped after Norbert.

Their jumps took them directly over the prison wall and they were falling towards the sea when suddenly the flying machine came beneath them and a hatch opened in the roof and the three cats fell through it. Then the machine closed the hatch and turned and flew in the direction it had come.

Inside Norbert just got to his feet ... right before Snow and Flame landed on their bottoms on top of him with an enormous thud.

'Goodbye horrible world!' wailed Flame.

'No more robberies for us!' wailed Snow.

'I love you, Snow, you are one in a million friend' wailed Flame.

'I love you too Flame you were one in a trillion friend' wailed Snow.

Then they both wailed together, 'But we can't say anymore because now we are gonna die!'

'Die!'

'Die!'

After that they both opened one eye and peeked around and then opened their other eye.

'Hey we are alive!' exclaimed Flame.

'We are!' exclaimed Snow. Then he looked around and said 'Hey! Where's Norbert?'

'Right below you two idiots!' growled Norbert.

'Gee sorry' said Flame as he and Snow climbed off Norbert.

'Well, look who is here?' said a voice coming from somewhere behind. The trio turned and saw a black Abyssinian cat standing in front of them.

'Night!' exclaimed Snow and Flame and ran to hug him.

'Don't forget us!' mewed another voice and two cats emerged, one sandy coloured with a small tinge of green from his shoulders to halfway down his back Siberian cat followed by a grey Sphynx cat.

'Leaf! Shorty!' exclaimed Snow and Flame and ran to hug them both.

Then Norbert smiled and said, 'It is a pleasure to meet you again Blacksmith tool scum, Green sand scum and Short stuff scum' which left Night, Leaf and Shorty very puzzled.

'How dare you laugh at my name!' yelled Shorty and he ran forward with a paw outstretched and tried to hit Norbert but Norbert calmly grabbed hold of his paw and twisted it. Hard.

'Ouch! My paw' exclaimed Shorty hopping around in pain

'What is Norbert on with these nicknames?' whispered Leaf.

'Until we prove that we are not terrible he will call us by them' whispered back Snow.

'Have you seen our employer yet?' asked Flame.

'Not yet but he promised to show himself to us as soon as we get to Paris' answered Night.

'Paris, we are going to Paris?' asked Snow in surprise.

'Yes, London isn't safe for us anymore so we have to immigrate, friend' answered Leaf.

'Goody! I have always wanted to travel and I can't wait to steal over there' yelled Flame in glee.

'What is this machine anyway?' asked Norbert stepping forward.

'It is called a plane. Our employer built it and he controls it from there,' answered Night pointing at a wooden door at the end of the room.

The room in which the cats were standing also was made up of wood and there was nothing in it which gave the cats lot of space.

'Do you at least know the name of our employer?' asked Norbert.

'Yes we do' answered Shorty. 'His name is the Valiant and Vicious Stryker'.

As he said this a noise came from outside and Snow went over to the window and said, 'Uh Oh! We have company!'

Flame also went with him and saw three boats coming from the prison towards them. 'Three boats are coming towards the plane' said Flame nervously and everyone except Norbert came to see.

'I don't want to be caught when I have already been freed' wailed Snow.

'Fluffy cloud scum, stop behaving like a coward and think of a plan' ordered Norbert.

'All our minds are too scared to think. Please you think of one' begged Flame.

Norbert sighed and was thinking when he heard a big wave coming in front of them. An idea came into his head. 'Stryker' he called.

'There is a big wave ahead so fly down to it and at the last minute fly up.' He heard no response but he saw his commands were being carried out as the plane flew down towards the wave with the boats in hot pursuit.

The plane immediately flew up as soon as the wave was upon them and the wave hit the boats instead. Looking back out of the window Norbert saw one of the boats had been flung upside down and the person in it was swimming towards the prison but the other two boats were still in pursuit.

He looked out of the front window and saw one big rock below them which was approaching. He called out 'Stryker go down again and fly towards the rock and then do what you did with the wave'.

He felt the plane going down and going at a high speed towards the rock and the boats closing in but as they reached the rock Stryker turned up in such a way that the cats were sent sprawling to the back of the room.

As he got up Norbert saw that one of the boats had crashed into the rock with the person inside having jumped out but the third boat was still after them and Norbert couldn't see any more waves or rocks. Then he got another brainwave and said, 'Stryker, go down right in front of the boat and then reverse and break it with the plane tail!'

The plane went down right in front of the boat and it reversed and destroyed the boat with the person quickly jumping out. Then the plane flew up and continued into the clouds.

'Yes! We got rid of all the boats and no one can stop us now' said Norbert, gleefully.

Chapter 3

Off to Paris

'That was a good lesson we had today' said Simon happily as he went along with Nick and Francis towards the cafeteria for their lunch break.

'Yeah from tomorrow we start to learn advanced gadgets' said Nick.

'I hope they have good sardines in the cafeteria. Last time the sardines were as horrible as ten cucumbers together!' said Francis.

Actually the cafeteria not only had good sardines there was also good meat and kippers and the three friends sat down to a good lunch.

'It has been a while since we had a mission' said Nick munching on his steak.

'Yeah ever since we caught Mr. Disguises and his lousy assistant, there hasn't been a mission for us spies' said Francis chewing on a sardine.

'I kind of wish there was an escaped convict and they choose us to get him or her' said Simon.

'Let's worry about missions later, there is a big test on what we have learnt so far in Spy class next week' said Nick.

'If we do well in this test we can move up higher things and get promoted to Detective class before we know it' said Simon.

'Yes, to think just a month ago we were Scouts and after catching a famous trio we are Spies' said Francis.

They talked for some more time over lunch and after some time they prepared to return to class when a brown and white cat came up to them. Ever since Francis and Simon had helped in catching the trio of cat burglars, the Detective and Spy House Agency had opened up to cats (the ones who hated mice of course) and even a cat High Council member had been installed.

'Excuse me' the cat spoke, 'Are you Nick, Francis and Simon?'

'Yes we are' answered Simon.

'Well, the High Council wants some of your time so can you spare some?' she continued.

'Of course' answered Francis, surprised.

'Okay see you' said the cat and she began to walk away but after a few steps she turned back and said, 'By the way I am lucky to meet you.' Saying that she happily ran off.

'Wow! I didn't know we were so popular over here,' exclaimed Simon.

'Yes I am happy to hear that as well but come on let us go to the High Council meeting hall' said Nick.

As they went towards the chamber they began to discuss why they had been called.

'We haven't done anything wrong' said Nick.

'Maybe it is another mission' said Simon smiling.

'Maybe Oh! Look we are at the chamber. Let us find out ourselves' said Francis.

The rabbit guard opened the door and they went into the chamber which was decorated with beautiful flowers around the walls. There were five desks in the centre of the room. At the centre was a wolfhound and on one side there was a mouse and a she-dove and on the other side there was a she-rabbit and a black and brown cat who was the new member.

'Greetings you three' spoke the wolfhound. 'I am sure you must be wondering why we have called you?'

'Yes why did you?' asked Francis.

'You remember catching Norbert, Snow and Flame?' asked the mouse.

'Yes, suffering badly in prison right now, I guess' said Nick.

'Apparently they were busted out of jail last night' continued the mouse.

Simon gasped and exclaimed 'What!'

'How in the world did they possibly do that?' asked Nick equally taken aback as Simon.

'Apparently they found an employer who took his plane and flew to the prison and freed the three cats' the dove started speaking.

'Well do you know where they are now?' asked Francis who looked the most taken aback.

'Yes our intel managed to track the plane to Paris' continued the dove.

'Well, what do you want us for? Why did you call us?' questioned Nick.

'That is easy' said the cat 'We are sending you to Paris to catch them'.

'Why us?' asked Nick.

'If you could catch them once you can always catch them again' continued the cat.

'Yes but can't you send someone else more experienced?' asked Francis.

'Yes we can but we think you will be ideal for the job' said the rabbit.

'But the classes are getting interesting and we have a test next week which we can't afford to miss' protested Simon.

'Do not worry your test can be postponed by us' said the rabbit.

'Guess we have no choice' sighed Nick 'But how are we going to get to Paris?'

'Like them, in a plane' answered the wolfhound. Then he turned to the mouse and asked, 'Will you escort them to the lab so that they can get going?'

'Sure' answered the mouse and he began to lead them out of the door.

'We shall inform your adopted parents Jacob and Mary about this' called out the dove behind them.

Nick, Francis and Simon had never been in the lab before and they were astounded by the size of the room and the number of computers and animals in there.

There were mice, doves, dogs and a few rabbits and cats who were all working on computers in the corners except for one dove who was at the biggest computer in the middle of the room.

The mouse walked up to that dove and asked, 'Is the plane ready?'

'Yes it is' answered the dove. 'It is our first plane and it is the fastest in the world'.

'These three Spies need it for a mission in Paris' said the mouse.

'Spies but they need to be top rank to go abroad!' said the dove surprised.

'Well, this mission can only be done by these three' protested the mouse.

'Sorry but they need to be three ranks up to go to Paris' said the dove firmly.

'Do you know who I am?' asked the mouse.

'Just a regular mouse over here' answered the dove.

'Not just any mouse, I am the one from the High Council and if you don't let these three on I shall fire you' threatened the mouse.

The dove immediately turned pale and shouted 'Ready the plane!'

A door opened in one corner of the room and behind it stood a plane. It was brown in colour and was a bit dirty but it still looked nice and a name was written on the side "Sky King".

'Bit rusty but nice' complimented Simon.

'Get on and I shall show you the controls' said the dove.

Nick and Francis jumped in immediately but as Simon went in the mouse stopped him and said, 'You can't go!'

'Why?' asked Simon.

'You got here only last month and you won't be experienced' answered the mouse.

'But I want to go' protested Simon.

'Sorry but I am a High Council mouse and I order you to get off' ordered the mouse.

Simon thought for a minute and asked, 'Can I just say one thing?'

'Sure' answered the mouse.

Simon reached down and whispered something into his ear.

'H-How di-did you know?' stammered the mouse as Simon finished whispering

'I am a know all' answered Simon.

'Well! I wish you and your friends a good mission and of course you can go, Simon' said the mouse.

Nick and Francis looked at each other in confusion as Simon settled himself in his seat with a big grin over his face.

'I will explain the controls now' said the dove he pointed to a lever and said, 'Pull it up to go up and push it down to go down.'

Then he pointed to two green buttons and said, 'Press the one on the left to go left and the one on the right to go right'.

Then he pointed to a blue and yellow button and said, 'Use that only in case of emergencies!'

Then he showed them one last red button in between the two which was enclosed in a glass hatch and had a warning below that said **DANGER DO NOT PUSH** and said, 'Whatever happens do not press that button! I repeat, do not press it. Think you can remember them?'

'Yes we can' answered Nick, confidently.

'Get ready for take-off' said the dove and a big hole opened up above the plane flooding Nick, Francis and Simon in the warm afternoon light. Francis pulled the lever up and the plane slowly started to go up.

'How long shall it take to reach Paris?' asked Simon.

'As this is the fastest plane in the world it shall only take two hours,' called the dove behind them.

Two and a half hours later the plane was slowly entering the harbour of London with the passengers on board very bored and annoyed. The plane must have never been tested before because it was very slow. The plane kept making a *dinghy* sound and every time the propellers made one circle a puft of smoke was released from the back.

'Forget *Sky King* this plane should be called *Sky Loser*' said Simon annoyed.

'Yes if this plane raced against a tortoise, the tortoise would win every time' said Francis feeling the same way.

'I wouldn't be surprised if we reached Paris by next week!' said Nick grouchily.

Chapter 4

In Paris

After one whole day the trio landed in Paris. They landed behind an abandoned factory and after hiding the plane they started to discuss their next movement.

'So now we need to find out where Norbert and the others are and make a plan to get hold of them' said Francis.

'We need to find a trail' said Nick.

'I know one such trail' said Simon.

'What?' asked Nick and Francis at the same time.

'If they are going to steal then we can ask someone about recent robberies' answered Simon.

'Good thinking, Simon' complimented Nick. 'Let us go and find someone in the city to help us.'

They walked out on the street and gazed around at the city. Paris had small buildings and rough streets like London and the only difference they could find was that the streets weren't as crowded as London and things were pleasanter.

'Look at that tower!' exclaimed Simon.

Nick and Francis looked and saw an enormous tower. Though it was at a considerable distance from them, it was very big and its top nearly touched the sky.

'It is very big indeed!' exclaimed Francis.

'Yes maybe we should go there once, but I wonder what it is called?' asked Nick.

'It is called the Eiffel Tower my friend' said a voice from behind them. They turned and saw a big Dalmatian walking towards them.

'It is so big some think if they go to the top they will be able to touch the sky' he continued.

'Thank you for telling us' said Francis.

'Can we ask you something?' asked Nick.

'On one condition' said the dog.

'What?' asked Simon.

The dog held out a flyer to Simon who took it and started reading it out to the others, 'THE 7TH ANNUAL BOWLING COMPETITION DAY HAS FINALLY ARRVED, THOSE WHO WISH TO PARTICIPATE MUST

REGISTER AT TOM'S ALLEY BY NOON ON 14TH MARCH. EVERYONE IS ALLOWED TO PARTICIPATE AND THE WINNER GETS A CHOICE OF THEIR FAVOURITE FOOD AND A DOZEN BOWLING BALLS GOOD LUCK TO EVERYONE. SIGNED IGO, HEAD OF THE BOWLING COMPANY'.

'What has this got to do everything?' asked Francis.

'I thought about entering but I injured my paw and I can't bowl so I want you to enter for me and if you win I shall answer any question of yours' said the dog

'We shall help you' assured Nick.

'Thank you' said the dog.

'I just remembered that today is 14th March' said Simon.

'What is the time right now?' asked Francis suddenly.

Simon looked at the clock of a nearby building and saw it was half an hour before noon. 'We have only half an hour to reach Tom's alley' he answered.

'Hurry!' cried Nick. 'We might just reach in time'

'I know the way' said the dog and they all started running, 'I am Boris by the way.'

They managed to reach Tom's alley as the clock struck and only one minute before twelve was left. They saw a kind looking dog behind a crate and quickly went over to her.

'We'd like to register, I am Nick, he is Francis and he is Simon' said Nick.

'Sure' answered the dog.

Boris decided to wait outside and so the others went over and joined a large group of animals.

Simon looked around and pointed to a black dog and said, 'He is Lord Spinner three times winner of the Bowling World Cup.' Then he pointed to a beautiful grey and white she-cat and said, 'She is Lady Paws, also three times winner of the Bowling Cup'.

'I can't believe we are meeting such big stars!' cried Francis joyfully.

'Shh!' shushed a cat next to him, 'Igo is about to speak.'

As he said this a big old grey Burmese cat appeared on one of the rooftops of a building in which the alley was enclosed and started to speak 'Bonjour participants!'

Loud cheers rang among the animals below. 'Welcome to the 7th Annual Bowling

Competition, I am sure that you all are very excited!' More cheers rang out.

'I am happy to see your eager faces for the grand prize which is food of your favourite choice and a Dozen bowling balls. Now enough talking and time to explain the rules first: we shall have single bowling rounds where everyone will only get one try and at the end we shall see that the ones with the best scores can go to round two. In round two everyone will be paired with someone and each team member shall only throw only once again. Three teams from there can advance to the finals and then it is single again and after that we shall calculate everyone's scores and we shall have our winner! *Bonne chance tous*'.

As he said this, Igo disappeared from view and the dog at the registration desk came in front of everyone carrying a tray with folded up chits containing every participant's name.

'Now I shall take one chit and see who goes first and after that who goes next and so on' she said and then without looking into the tray, she moved one paw around and started rummaging around. Her paw finally took one and she opened it and read out, 'Nick!'

'Me?' stammered Nick in surprise.

'Come on, go show them' encouraged Francis.

With great nervousness, Nick went towards the bowling area. The area was in front of the exit of the alley and there was only one small plastic ball and few metres away from it were ten empty milk bottles as bowling pins. Nick took up the ball with both his paws and he tried to throw as best as he could. The ball slowly started to roll towards the pins, he closed his eyes as he heard some splintering sound. After a minute he opened them and saw that three pins were still standing but seven had been hit and were lying broken.

As he went back to his place he saw two cats come near the pins and one of them, with a broom and dustpan began to sweep up the broken pieces while the other put seven other milk bottles in its place. Then the first went over to the ball and put it in its place then they both disappeared from sight.

The dog again rummaged around in the tray and picked up a chit and called out, 'Lady Paws!' Lady Paws smiled and went over to the ball and picked it up then she threw the ball and it began to roll faster and faster and it hit the bottles and broke every last one.

'Strike!' called an unseen voice.

Lady Paws smiled and went back to her place as the two cats from before did what they were supposed to do and then the dog called out the next contestant. After a few more contestants, the dog called out, 'Francis!' and Francis went out towards the ball.

He picked up the ball and was about to throw it when he slipped and the ball went flying towards the right wall from where it ricocheted onto the left wall, then again to the right and then once more to the left, and then up into the air. Falling down it bounced off Francis's head and started rolling and broke every last bottle.

'Strike!' called the unseen voice.

After two more contestants came and went the dog called out, 'Lord Spinner!' and the big dog went over to the ball and picked it up. Everyone saw that his name was not Spinner for nothing as he picked up the ball with his two paws and spun it around then he threw it and the ball started to go spinning rapidly towards the milk bottles and it was a strike. He smiled and went back to his place as the next contestant was called out.

After many more contestants came it was finally Simon's turn. He went putting a bold face on and picked up the ball and rolled it and it managed to break eight out of the ten bottles and he went back to his place. Everyone watched the remaining contestants take their turns and after the last one the dog came out with a list of everyone who had managed to qualify for the next round.

Nick was relieved to hear that he and Francis and Simon had managed to reach the next round and so had Lord Spinner and Lady Paws. The dog called out to the disappointed animals who hadn't managed to qualify and said, 'No need to be upset, you can go and watch the rest of the game with Igo' which brightened up everyone.

The two cleaner cats beckoned the animals to follow them and off they went. The dog took out a second list and said, 'Now I shall tell everyone who you are partnered with.' Saying that she began to read out from the list.

'Jackson and Hobbs' 'Marie and Annie' and so on then she read out 'Lord Spinner and Lady Paws' 'Nick and Simon' and at the end she read out 'Francis and Ettie'. Then she folded up the list and walked away as everyone tried to find their partners.

Lord Spinner and Lady Paws found each other easily and so did Nick and Simon. A she-rat walked up to Francis and asked, 'Are you Francis?'

'Yes I am,' he answered.

'I am Ettie,' said the she-rat.

'Nice to meet you' said Francis, but deep inside he was thinking, "We are up against many competitors including two three time World Cup winners and none of us three have any experience! What is gonna happen!"

Chapter 5

The Semis and the Finals

All right, time for the team bowling. After both the teams hit the bottles, we shall count the score and decide which team progresses' called out the dog.

'First Hobbs and Jackson against Marie and Annie' as she said this a mouse and dog came out as well as a she-cat and she-dog.

'You are going down!' yelled the mouse.

'We shall see about that' challenged back the she-cat.

It began with the she-cat and dog going first, the cat picked up the ball and rolled it and seven bottles broke and fell. The cleaner cats came again and swept up the mess and put new bottles. Then the dog picked them up and rolled the ball and it broke nine bottles.

After the new bottles had been put, the mouse from the other team went first. He of course could not pick up the ball so he ran and hit the ball with his side and it rolled and broke half of the bottles. Then the dog rolled the ball and it shot forward and did a strike!

'Jackson and Hobbs win' said the dog and they went off with smiles on their faces while Marie and Annie went away with a dejected look.

Next it was Francis and Ettie against two toms who looked big and strong. Francis went first and picked up the ball and rolled it. But he must have thrown it a bit high because it flew and hit the lamppost on the other side of the street but then miraculously, it flew up and landed on the lamppost on the street behind them. Then it flew and did a bounce in front of Francis and started rolling and it was a strike again.

Then Ettie went next, Francis saw her run and hit the ball with super mouse strength and rolled and shot down and it was a strike. The two toms went but they could not match Francis and Ettie's score and Francis and Ettie progressed ahead.

After a few more contestants it was Nick and Simon's turn. They both were up against one cat and one big dog. The cat went first, it took up the ball and rolled it fast. It shot down faster than you could say "slow" and knocked down nine out of the ten bottles.

Smiling, he went back to his place while the dog went forward and rolled the ball faster than the cat and knocked eight out of ten bottles.

'It won't be easy to beat them,' whispered Nick to Simon as Simon went out and took his place and got ready. Putting on his bold face again he went forward, picked up the ball and rolled it. The ball started to roll slowly at first but began to gain more speed as it went and knocked down every bottle that was standing. It was a strike!

'Knock down at least eight of the pins and we progress ahead' whispered Simon to Nick as he went and took his place near the ball. He picked it up and rolled it as fast as he could while he silently wished for it too knock down eight of the bottles and he was relieved when he saw that he had not knocked down eight but had gotten a strike as well which meant he and Simon could progress ahead.

Then it was Lord Spinner and Lady Paws against two dogs named Quentin and George. Quentin went first and rolled the ball with all he had and knocked down half of the bottles.

After a minute George went ahead and with slow motion picked up the ball and rolled it and knocked down eight bottles and he took his place. Then Lady Paws went and picked up the ball and gracefully swung it and rolled the ball and it was a strike and Lord Spinner also had the same result.

'They are going to be tough opponents if we come face to face' whispered Francis to Ettie.

'Don't worry with your gift we can easily beat them' said Ettie.

'My gift?' echoed Francis.

'Of course all these skills are a gift to you' said Ettie. 'Oh! Look they have called our name it is time for us to play again!' So they went out in the field and continued to progress ahead and along with them Nick and Simon continued to do so too.

So at the end of the team bowling the three teams who would be moving into the final were announced, 'Nick and Simon, Lord Spinner and Lady Paws, and Francis and Ettie'

'Well we have a 1 on 1 chance to win' said Simon to Nick.

'Yes but two of them are world champions so it is not gonna be that easy' said Nick.

'Well Francis it was nice playing with you but now I have to play against you so all the best!' said Ettie.

'All the best to you too' called Francis out after her.

During the break they talked to each other about how to find Norbert, Snow and Flame.

'Even if we win Paris is a big city so it will be very difficult to find them' said Nick.

'Yes we were chosen specially by the High Council so we can't let them down' said Francis.

'Indeed but how are we going to capture them and their employer?' asked Simon.

'Well, we were sent with a few gadgets so those should do' answered Francis.

'I wonder what will happen if we don't win and we won't get any information' said Nick.

'Yes but there are many other animals we can ask them' said Simon.

'How did we get ourselves in this mess?' asked Francis.

'We can't turn away from the mission. We will surely get them' promised Nick.

Just then they heard the shout that signalled the start of the final round of the tournament. As they went they heard the dog say, 'Okay Igo decided to make this round a bit difficult so here you are!'

Everyone turned their heads and saw that the floor of the bowling had now been applied with oil making it slippery.

'My! Everybody's chances of winning are going a bit low' remarked Francis.

'Okay first Ettie' cried the dog.

Francis watched his former partner go pick up the ball and roll it but because of the slippery surface the ball went spinning and sliding here and there and in the end only knocked down three bottles.

Ettie walked off dejected as Lord Spinner's name was called and he proudly went to take his place. He picked up the ball and spun it three times and rolled it but the ball kept sliding and missed the bottles all together! He fell to the ground and started wailing, 'No! It can't be!' and wailing loudly he walked off dejected.

Then Simon's name was called out. He boldly picked up the ball and rolled it as best as he could it kept changing but ultimately hit four bottles. Nick was next and he rolled the ball and knocked only two bottles down.

Then Lady Paws was called out. She gracefully picked up the ball and rolled it went sliding but however it knocked down six bottles.

'Come on Francis you have to win' requested Nick.

'I will try my best' assured Francis as he stepped out and picked up the ball and rolled it. However like in his previous turns the ball instead flew up and bounced off the walls and hit the wall at the other end of the street , then flew up and hit on the other side of the street. The ball then started spinning faster and faster it came but as soon as it got into the oil the ball suddenly caught on fire because of the friction and the oil.

However, the ball was not thrown off its path and continued now completely on fire towards the bottles and it was a strike once again. The inferno rolled down the streets of Paris but nobody paid much attention to it as they were now murmuring in excitement.

Suddenly Igo stepped in front of Francis and looked at him with interest in his eyes. 'What's your name he asked?'

'Fr-Fra-Francis' he stammered because he was thrilled to be in front of a famous cat.

'Not anymore you shall now be known as Francis the Fireball in honour of your fiery ball' he said and immediately everyone erupted and chanted 'The Fireball! The Fireball!'

'I am pleased' said Francis.

'Yes felicitations' said Igo. 'Now for your prize what food would you like?'

'Some meat please' requested Francis.

'Very well' said Igo and he clapped his paws and a small sack was carried and dropped at Francis's feet and a box containing the bowling balls was also dropped.

'We have our winner!' cried Igo as the crowd erupted once more.

Boris came walking up. 'Thanks for winning I will be outside' he said before walking away as Lady Paws came up.

'Good job I have never seen someone as good as you until today. I have to admit I am a bit jealous' she said.

Lord Spinner also came over and said with tears marks on his cheeks 'I am sniff very pleased sniff for you!'

Nick and Simon then came over. 'You were very good today maybe you should teach others' said Nick.

'Good job cuz' complimented Simon.

'Come on let us go to Boris now' said Francis and they all went out through the excited crowd and met Boris.

'Here is your prize' said Nick as they handed over the bag.

'Thank you by the way you can keep the bowling balls if you like I have no use for them' he said.

On seeing this the crowd murmured, 'Ooh! He is so generous he gives his prize to another!'

'Right so now what do you want to know?' asked Boris.

'Well have there been robberies around here lately?' asked Simon.

Boris looked surprised at such a question but he said, 'Yes only one last night a nearby house was robbed and some jewels were stolen. I heard this from some friends of mine'.

'Well was anyone seen around at that time' asked Francis.

'Oh! Yes three cats were seen walking shortly afterwards' Boris said which got the trio's attention.

'Do you know what the cats looked like?' asked Nick.

'Yes one was a black Abyssinian cat another was a Siberian cat with a sandy colour and green tinge up to his back and a grey Sphynx cat'

'Oh!' said Nick sounding disappointed that it wasn't the cats they were looking for.

'Anyway I will be off' said Boris as he walked away leaving the trio staring hopeless in the dust.

Chapter 6

New Plans

Meanwhile hidden in the depths of the dumps of Paris, Norbert and his gang were resting inside the plane and were thinking of the coming night robbery. Okay it was an exaggeration on that part, only Norbert was relaxing while the others were, let us see what they were doing.

'Stupid ginger scum hurry up with the cleaning! And Fluffy cloud scum I am thirsty! Where is my milk?!'

'Coming' cried Snow as he carried a tray with wobbly paws and a bowl of milk on it up to the roof of the plane where Norbert was sitting on a chair found in the dump.

'Here you are' he said and gave the tray to him which he in turn took up the bowl in his two paws and gulped the milk down in one gulp.

'Good' he said licking his whiskers. 'Run down to Short stuff scum and ask him if my lunch is ready yet and ask Blacksmith tool scum on the way if the weapons I asked for are ready'

'Yes' answered Snow and quickly ran down.

Norbert turned to look at Flame who was cleaning near the opening of the roof and said, 'Hey how you doing?'

'Fine' answered Flame. 'By the way with the cleaning my appetite has worked up lot of hunger so can I get something to eat?'

'Sure' said Norbert and he took out a steel canister of soup and threw it. It hit Flame on the head which made him lose his balance and fall through the opening and into the plane and the canister fell in and hit Flame on the head again which knocked him out.

'Next time wait until I say you can eat then eat' said Norbert (though Flame didn't hear because he was still knocked out).

Just then he spotted a streak across the sky 'Green sand scum and Stryker returning' thought Norbert. He had sent them to spy on more houses and find one ideal for that night. They landed on the roof and Leaf got off Stryker.

Stryker it turned out was a huge hawk with sharp talons and his beak was also very sharp and he had a small mark on his cheek.

'Find any good houses?' asked Norbert.

'Yes one with lot of jewels' answered Stryker.

'Good go back and investigate and report back' ordered Norbert.

'Right away' said Leaf and got back on Stryker and flew off. Norbert smiled and relaxed back in his chair and thought that nothing could get better than this. He wondered if someone from the Detective and Spy House Agency had discovered their escape and sent someone after them. Well, whoever it was they would dish them out and continue to steal.

Just then he heard some voices below. He peeked over and saw five cats come towards the plane and upon seeing it start murmuring among themselves. He jumped in the hatch and climbed down the staircase built for his food and drinks to be carried up and met the cats outside.

A cat with black spots and a ginger body said, 'Are you the occupant of this plane?'

'Indeed I am' answered Norbert.

'Well your plane is on top of a hole which is kind of where we stay so can you get it off?' requested the cat.

'Why would I?' challenged Norbert. 'The plane is going to be here for some time so find somewhere else whatever your name is'.

'It is Hart' said the cat. He pointed to a cream coloured cat with brown ears and said, 'That is my mate Hilda.'

Then he pointed to a cat with a black and white body and with only two whiskers on each side and said, 'That is my son Whisker' and then he pointed to a black and brown and an apple red cat and said, 'Those are my daughters Yellow and Pink.'

'Okay you can find somewhere else to live cause we aren't budging' said Norbert rudely. 'Please my father and his father and in fact our family has lived in that hole for generations' pleaded Hart.

'Well you will have to fight for it' said Norbert.

'Okay you asked for it all of you attack!' cried Hart.

'All of you get ready for battle!' cried Norbert but nobody responded. It wasn't surprising because Flame was still unconscious and

Snow had not returned yet from Night and Shorty who were doing their jobs and Leaf and Stryker were still investigating so Norbert was pushed back trying to block all the types of blows coming towards him. He was pushed onto the plane and was being pushed up the staircase just then Yellow singled out and attacked him and Norbert saw his chance and overpowered her and ran many scratches over her.

He would have loved to scratch more but the other cats were advancing and he had to do something fast, he banged Yellow's head five times against the stairs and giving one heavy blow himself he pushed her over the staircase where she lay limp and her head bleeding heavily.

The others pushed him up towards the terrace as Hart came in and checked Yellow's heart which wasn't beating so he growled and followed the others up. Up on the terrace Norbert was attacked by Hilda who sat on top of him and scratched his belly with her claws. Whisker and Pink also moved in.

Thinking fast Norbert kicked up with his hind legs which sent Hilda flying and he heard her hit a pile of junk. He knew that pile was full of hard things and if you hit your skull hard against them that would be the end of you. Whisker and Pink quickly ran over there and Norbert followed their gaze and saw Hilda lying with her eyes staring blankly and without light.

Whisker howled in anger and leaped at Norbert but Norbert was ready for him and caught him and overpowered him. He hit him hard on the head three times and pushed him over the edge of the plane as Pink leaped at him and before he leaped into battle Norbert saw Hart arrive on the terrace as Pink landed on him and Norbert was trying to fend her off.

She tried to aim a killing bite at his throat but he narrowly avoided it and bit into her shoulder. Then he held her tight and ran his claws over her throat and she fell on the terrace coughing up blood as Norbert turned to face Hart.

'How dare you take so many lives from me!' he growled.

'Well come fight and try to avenge them' challenged back Norbert.

Hart growled again and both of them leaped at each other at the same time and both started rolling on the terrace. Norbert felt at a stinging scratch above his eye as Hart slashed at it but Norbert ran his front paws over Hart's pelt. Suddenly the ground disappeared from beneath them and they hit against it a few seconds later and Norbert realised they were falling down the steps and when they landed, they fell apart from each other.

As Norbert was getting up he saw Whisker limp in and directed his attention on him. He leaped on Whisker and they both fell outside the plane, Norbert immediately saw that Whisker was an easy target because his blows and falling off the edge of the plane had weakened him. Norbert held him down and sank his teeth into his throat and left him to die and trudged back inside where Hart was waiting for him.

'Let's end this once and for all' said Hart and they leaped at each other again. This time Hart pounded heavier on him and Norbert soon was being overpowered when he suddenly got a brainwave. He kicked out with his hind paws and knocked Hart's front feet from beneath him and slowly this gave Norbert the upper hand. He grabbed hold of Hart and started bashing his head against the wall, he didn't know how long it had been but Norbert found that he enjoyed it and continued bashing Hart's head on the wall.

'Norbert, what are you doing?' asked a voice. He turned around and saw Flame getting up and rubbing his sore head with one paw looking puzzled. Norbert then turned and saw Hart's head was a bloody mess and now he was still in his arms and not moving, his amber eyes staring up at him.

He let the body drop on the floor as Flame noticed it and Yellow's body nearby and asked again 'What were you doing? Why did you kill them?!'

Just then Snow poked his head in with Night and Shorty behind him and said, 'Both of them are ready with what you asked but on the way here I saw a cat lying dead in the rubbish heap and one lying just outside, was it you who did it?'.

Just then he heard some movement on the terrace and Stryker and Leaf came in.

'We found the best way to enter the house but up on the terrace as we came back we saw a dead cat. Was it you who killed her?' asked Stryker.

Then Norbert erupted. 'Yes! Yes! It was me! These filthy cats were trying to move our plane but I wouldn't let them! And instead of asking me questions all of you back to work! Stupid ginger scum continue cleaning! Fluffy cloud scum go clean the cockpit! Stryker you and Blacksmith tool scum bury these bodies 10 metres in the ground! Green sand scum go down to the engines and I heard mice down there so kill every last one! And now I am going to eat and then Short stuff scum every plate thrice!' thundered Norbert.

Then he shouted one more thing, 'I shall not let Team Cat fall under the hands of idiots!'

'Team Cat?' echoed everyone.

'Of course all gangs have a name! Any problem?' asked Norbert.

'Uh, not at all' replied everyone hastily and scuttled back to their jobs.

Chapter 7

A Night Chase

That evening the trio were sitting down to a light supper consisting of some rubbish found in some bins. 'I can't believe we are no closer to finding those criminals' said Nick as he bit into an apple.

'Yes the only robbery took place last night and there was no trace of them at all' said Francis biting into some fish remains.

Simon who was having some potato sticks said, 'Come on guys don't give up hope. I am sure we will be on them sooner or later.'

'Yes but how long is it gonna take, huh?' said Francis.

'I wonder what are we gonna do?' said Nick 'Good apple by the way but we should have brought some food with us'.

'Hey! I just had a thought!' said Francis suddenly.

'What?' echoed Nick and Simon.

'What if those three cats were actually friends of Norbert and the others?' asked Francis excitedly.

'Now that is a thought! Yes, it could be true' said Nick.

'Wait! I just had a better idea' said Simon.

'What is it?' asked Francis.

'Those thieves will only steal at night' stated Simon.

'Yes so?' asked Nick.

'We have our gliders and all,' said Simon thoughtfully.

'Yes so?' asked Nick again.

'Oh! Come on, that bit is obvious' said Simon.

A couple of hours later Francis was flying over a certain part of Paris with his glider and a walkie talkie strapped to his glider.

'Agent Francis, this is Agent Nick, any sign? Over.'

'Nothing, Agent Nick, as yet. Over.' said Francis over the walkie talkie.

The plan of Simon had been simple. Each of them would cover a certain part of the city for any sign of criminal activity by Norbert and the others and they could talk with each other through the walkie talkie. Francis glanced around but there was still no sign.

He glanced up to where the giant Eiffel Tower stood. One of the places he wanted to go to in Paris was that tower maybe, something would eventually bring him to the tower. He looked at the dark sky above him. Right now he felt as if he could fly without the hang glider, stay under water for ten minutes and survive, he felt as if he owned the night.

Shaking himself from his fantasy, he glanced around and saw that there was still no sign, well some more fantasies wouldn't hurt. He then thought that when they had successfully caught the cats and sent them back to prison he would be promoted to Detective rank along with Nick and Simon.

He then thought that after a few successful missions, he would then be promoted to Field Agent and then he would reach the last rank. Ah! Life abroad would await him and what luxurious places he might be sent to!

He imagined the tropical region of Hawaii, or the pretty gardens of Japan or in Russia where daylight stayed for a long time or maybe even somewhere near the Himalayas where it was nice and cool. He then imagined that a pretty she-cat would come up to him and ask, 'Will you be my mate?' 'Yes' answered Francis aloud.

'Agent Francis come in. This is Agent Simon. Come in. Over.' Simon's loud voice shook awake from his nightdream (which is the opposite of daydream because this is at night).

'Nothing yet Agent Simon any luck? Over'.

'Nothing here either Agent Francis. Over.

Francis then suddenly got serious and started looking over for any sign of Norbert or anybody else. Just as he was about to ask Nick something, a movement at the corner of his eye caught his attention. He looked and saw one shadowy figure sitting on the terrace of a building calling out something though, the figure spoke so quietly Francis couldn't hear what was being said.

Then three other figures came out of the building at the bottom with one carrying a small sack. They looked up at the shadowy figure and some more words passed between them though it was too quiet again to hear. Then two shadowy heads peeked out of the top window and one of them threw a tiny rope which landed on the terrace. He climbed up the rope and the other carrying a small sack climbed up behind him. That was when the moonlight shone on them.

Francis saw that the shadowy figure was Norbert while the other two were Flame and Snow. He glanced down at the three cats below and saw that they were exactly like Boris had described so Simon had been right after all.

Silently he called to Nick, 'Agent Francis here, come in Agent Nick, I have spotted the criminals. Over.'

'This is Agent Nick, I am telling Agent Simon and we are coming to your aid. Hold them off in the meantime. Over.'

Francis then veered his glider and flew at them screaming 'Stop there in the name of the law!'

The cats turned to see him and there was a familiar recognition in Norbert, Snow and Flame's eyes.

'Night! Leaf! Shorty! Run!' screamed Norbert as the three cats below scuttled off into darkness and he with Snow and Flame behind him started jumping across the rooftops.

'What should I do? I can't chase after both parties' thought Francis.

Just then he spotted Nick and Simon flying to him.

'Just in time!' he called out.

'Where are they?' asked Simon quickly.

'Norbert and Snow and Flame went in that direction, and the three cats that were described to us were friends of theirs who ran off down below'.

'I will take care of Norbert and the other two while you and Nick catch those three cats' said Simon.

'Okay!' they called out and flew off into the darkness while Simon turned and chased after Norbert, Snow and Flame.

The air increased which gave a boost to Simon and allowed him to fly faster after Norbert and spot him and Snow and Flame only three rooftops away.

'Stop there you knuckleheads!' he cried.

Norbert turned around and glared at him and said, 'How dare you call us knuckleheads?! Fluffy cloud scum go get him!' and Snow leaped to do his bidding leaving the sack he was carrying with Norbert.

He jumped onto the next rooftop as Simon flew overhead and leaped at his legs. However, Simon moved his legs out of his reach and kicked at him. His kick was so hard that Snow was sent flying over the edge of the building but thankfully landed on a pile of mud in the middle of the road which broke his fall.

Norbert shook his head in despair and ordered, 'Stupid ginger scum! Go try again and be careful!'

Flame immediately leaped at Simon with fast reflexes and had better success then Snow as he caught hold of Simon's paws which held the glider making it unsteady.

However, Simon suddenly bit on Flame's shoulder and removed his paws and sent him flying like Snow over the edge of the building and making him land next to him in the mud pile.

Simon then turned to Norbert who was holding Snow's sack and said, 'Your game is over, Norbert give up!'

Norbert smiling said, 'I still have one last trick with me!'

Then he took out a small wooden ninja star from a small pouch on his side 'Blacksmith tool scum made these especially for me and this very rare wood which can cut through any metal'.

He raised his hand backward with the star and threw it at the still air-borne Simon, who immediately raised one of his front paws to shield himself while keeping a hold of the glider with the other. The blow never came.

'Hah! You missed' taunted Simon removing his paw from his face.

'I wasn't aiming for you' said Norbert and glanced at his glider. Simon turned and saw there was a big tear in the glider and he was starting to go down slowly.

'No!' he cried when suddenly a big gust of wind came towards him and sent him flying and tumbling in the air. After a few minutes of being tumbled the wind stopped and Simon was going down again at a rapid pace again.

Suddenly he saw he was going to crash into a big pile of junk stored up and arranged in neat rows some of which looked hard. 'No! No! No!' cried Simon as he crashed into the junk.

Meanwhile Nick and Francis were busy flying down a long street in pursuit of Night, Leaf and Shorty.

'I have an idea Francis' whispered Nick. 'You chase them down the next road and I will fly in from one end and you from the other and we will catch them'

'Good idea' whispered back Francis as Nick flew off. He tried to go as fast as possible with the mild breeze and slowly was nearly onto the three cats.

'You will enjoy prison life soon' he said as he saw Nick come in from the other side of the road and the three cats froze in the middle of the road with the advancing Nick and Francis coming.

However, Nick and Francis had not noticed a tiny alley which they could just squeeze themselves in and that's what the three cats did. They were in so fast that Nick and Francis could barely see them doing it and suddenly realised that they were still going towards each other at a fast pace. They suddenly crashed in the middle of the road and fell on the ground seeing nothing but stars for a few minutes.

The three cats came out and taunted them saying, 'Losers!' and quickly running off. After they were feeling better they got up and rubbed their heads.

'Man we were so close!' said a dismayed Nick.

'Don't worry those cats are too greedy to leave Paris just now' assured Francis.

Just then they heard an evil laugh above them and saw Norbert and the other cats standing on the building in front of them.

'Norbert your game is up' said Francis starting to get his glider ready.

'Not so fast' said Norbert and Snow and Flame came ahead carrying a black lump which Francis immediately saw was Simon! 'We have your cousin as a prisoner. We will spare him on the condition that you will no longer come after us in Paris for the nights to come or else you will find his tail posted to you' Then he and the other cats disappeared into the darkness of the night with Simon.

Chapter 8

A Test

'Don't worry Francis, I am sure Simon is okay' comforted Nick the next day as Francis sat at their base staring quietly into space.

'Nice try but they could be doing anything right now to him. Like what if they really cut off his tail or send us his ears?' said Francis not looking at Nick.

'Look I am troubled as just as much as you are' said Nick.

'No you are not!' cried Francis. He got up and trudged towards the street.

'Where are you going?' asked Nick.

'To try and find Simon or at least a clue as to where he is' spat Francis and before Nick could say anything else he was gone.

However it had been not more than a few minutes when Francis started walking when suddenly clouds covered the sky and in a few minutes there was a downpour of rain. The streets were now empty so he tried to find shelter but there was none and soon his fur was soggy and heavy.

Finally he saw a small shelter-like space between two dustbins and seeing no other choice went towards it and sat down waiting for the rain to clear. He shook himself dry and tried to lick the water off his fur as much as possible.

Ugh! He hated getting wet. As he sat there he started to think and thought that he might have been a bit too upset over Simon's capture. Then his bad mood returned and he realised that he truly had to find a clue of Simon and he would get started as soon as the rain stopped.

After what felt like a million light years the rain finally stopped and Francis walked out looking around and trying to avoid the many puddles which had been formed. He walked the streets while all he felt inside was a mixture of anger and sadness.

He had only been walking for a few minutes when he heard a voice behind him say, 'Hey! Hello, Francis the Fireball good day!' he turned around and saw that it was Boris who was standing right over there.

Taking a deep breath, he tried to calm himself down and answered 'Well I suppose it is a good day'.

'Where's Nick?'

'Back where we are staying'

'And Simon?'

Francis just said nothing and shrugged his shoulders 'I am not feeling fine today. I just feel very angry and upset' he said.

'Is it about Simon?' asked Boris.

'Yes but I don't feel like telling the details' said Francis.

Boris stood for a moment thinking. Then he stood up straight and said, 'I know someone who can help control your anger but the way it is done, well, it can be dangerous'.

Francis stared at him for a moment and then said, 'I don't care whether it is dangerous or not I am welcome to any help'.

'Well then follow me' said Boris.

He went down and Francis followed him as quickly as he could. He went down countless alleys and streets until Boris finally stopped in front of a dark looking alley.

'There go in' said Boris.

'Aren't you coming?' asked Francis.

'No, for this type of thing you have to go by yourself'

Francis took a deep breath and went inside the alley. He kept going and as he went in, it started to become slightly dark than before until finally at the end he saw an odd-looking dog.

The dog had a shawl drawn over his face and he couldn't tell what breed it was. Near the dog he could see bowls with strange looking mixtures. As he went close the dog looked up and growled in a deep voice 'Come. What do you want?'

Francis sat next to him and explained his problem.

'So do you have any idea what to do?' he asked in the end.

The dog was silent for a few minutes.

Then he spoke, 'Yes, to calm your anger you must go to the dream world and there you will face a test and if you win you shall be cured of your anger'.

'How do I get there?' asked Francis 'And what sort of test will I face?'

'Answers shall come in time and to get to the dream world just go to sleep and I will take care of the rest' said the strange dog.

Francis still had many questions to ask but he knew he must do as he said so he went down on the floor, closed his eyes and let himself fall into a deep sleep.

Francis had no idea where he was. The world around him was like a long tunnel and parts of it were blue and some were purple and there was only one starry road on which he was walking.

'Is this the dream world?' he wondered aloud.

He walked for a few minutes without seeing anybody or anyone. Finally he paused and said to himself, 'I don't understand! If this is the dream world why isn't there anybody around? And what is the test supposed to be? And how can I save Simon?'

'Oh! Your pathetic cousin!' came a familiar voice.

Francis turned and saw the unmistakable shape of none other than Norbert striding towards him. Francis felt anger rise inside him and he advanced forward. He could tell this Norbert wasn't real but he still felt nothing but anger on seeing him.

The dream Norbert came close to him and said, 'Come on too scared to attack me?'

'Shut up! You aren't real' snapped Francis.

'Oh! This is real enough' said the dream Norbert and as fast as lightning he was on him and sank his teeth into his shoulder.

The pain was searing! Francis recoiled, then he leaped for Norbert but as soon as he touched him, Norbert disintegrated into black smoke and Francis swiped at empty air.

'Where did he go?' Francis wondered to himself and he got his answer when he felt something bite down on his leg. He whipped around and saw the dream Norbert standing behind him.

'Too slow' he taunted as Francis leaped for his throat but as before the dream Norbert disintegrated into black smoke and Francis hit the ground. As he got up he felt claws raking along his pelt and the dream Norbert was standing next to him.

'What have you done with Simon?' demanded Francis.

'Oh! Your pathetic cousin I think I may have already cut of his tail' said the dream Norbert but as he finished Francis leaped for him again.

Again the dream Norbert vaporised into smoke and Francis sailed through and fell again on the path. The dream Norbert rematerialized a few feet away and taunted saying 'Too pathetic" and "I am getting tired of this charade".

Francis wanted to claw him again but he knew by now that if he attacked again the same thing would happen so he sat and thought for a minute, and realised that all the times he had attacked the dream Norbert he had attacked him in anger.

Taking a deep breath he knew it would be difficult to attack without anger but he had to try. He started walking towards Norbert trying to be calm. He thought of Nick that he was doing this for him and continued advancing.

'Come on show me your anger' said the dream Norbert mockingly but Francis took another deep breath and thought of when he had won the bowling tournament and how everyone had been chanting his name.

He continued walking towards the dream Norbert who was close now. As he was nearly there he thought of Simon. He was taking this test to help free him and he stopped in front of the dream Norbert who spoke up 'Come on be angry'

However Francis turned a deaf ear to that and swiped his paw at Norbert's jaw. As his paw came in contact with the dream Norbert, instead of vaporising into smoke he got shattered into tiny pieces which fluttered away.

Francis stood still not believing that he had won and as he stood panting the dream world started to become blurry and he woke up back in the real world in the dark alley. He inspected his shoulder and saw a small scratch on the brink of healing. So maybe his trip had been a little real as he stood up, his legs having a bit of a cramp inside them. As he did so the strange dog approached him and stood silently watching him as he got ready to leave.

Francis stopped and looked at him as well and after an eternity the dog nodded approvingly and said, 'Good job! You passed the test and in doing so you have gained a special power'.

'What is it?' asked Francis his eyes brightened up and full of curiosity.

'You will find out in time and I think you should go now' promised the dog.

Francis still had many questions but he walked towards the entrance and came out into the bright sunlight and noticed that it was nearly sunset and he saw Boris approaching him.

'So how did it go?' he asked.

'Fine' answered Francis. 'I thank you for bringing me here.'

'Don't mention it' said Boris. 'Anyway I should be heading home right now so see you soon'

He turned and jogged off. Francis realised he had to go back as well so as fast as his feet could take him he started running back.

Chapter 9

A Petite Escape Plan

'Ha! Excellent idea, trapping Francis's pathetic cousin and keep him hostage so that we are not bothered until we leave Paris' roared Stryker delightedly that night.

'Yes from tomorrow I will start torturing him to tell us about the Detective and Spy House Agency and by the time I am done with him he will be spitting out his tongue both figuratively and literally' cried Norbert. Then he smiled and said, 'In fact why don't I start right now?'

'Yes, nice idea' said Shorty coming from the cockpit.

'Take me to him Short stuff scum' ordered Norbert and he added, 'Don't comment on your nickname or else you will have another sprained paw.'

Shorty nodded and looked down at his paw which was wrapped in a small cloth. 'Come' he said and Norbert followed him outside the plane and through many hills of garbage to a dark corner of the dump where Simon was there wrapped up in bite proof and claw proof rope fastened by a thick padlock.

Snow and Flame were guarding him and upon seeing Norbert they said, 'Greetings, what do you need?'

'I need some time alone with him' answered Norbert.

'Okay' said both Snow and Flame and then they both left with Shorty following them.

'Right let us get to business' said Norbert smiling. 'Now let me ask you something what part would you like to keep? A claw or one ear?'

'Both' answered Simon shivering.

'No, be nice, now answer clearly would you like to keep a claw or an ear? If you don't answer I will cut off both!' threatened Norbert.

Simon looked petrified and shakily answered 'Every cat needs his ears!'

'Very well then one claw it is' said Norbert and he grabbed hold of one paw of Simon and unsheathed his claws and got ready.

'Please don't! Please don't!' begged Simon as Norbert's claws came closer and closer but just as they were extremely close they stopped and were sheathed again.

'Oh! Sorry! I am being rude. This is too extreme, let me start with the basics tonight' said Norbert looking as apologetic as he could. Then he grinned wickedly and unsheathed his claws again and said, 'Let us begin'.

Two hours later Norbert left and Night and Leaf were left to guard Simon. As they stood guard, Simon was still squirming from the pain and looked at his many scratches and wounds some of which would leave a scar. He had to escape that night he decided but first he had to get rid of Night and Leaf and open his bonds.

He shouted out 'Hey! I am thirsty!'

Night came answering to him and said, 'You already drank a few hours ago now next drin-' he was cut off as Simon managed to stretch one leg and trip him up and as Night went down he managed to head-butt him hard on the head and Night stumbled and fell unconscious.

Leaf came over there and he looked mad. He came closer and raised his paw to hit Simon when Simon bashed his own face in Leaf's face which knocked out Leaf at once. Now all he had to do was get out of his bonds and he knew just what to do. He heaved as much as he could to the padlock of his rope and raised his paw and took out a single claw and grinning put it into the lock and twisted and turned it around and soon the lock clicked open.

The ropes became loose and he wriggled his way out and carefully stepped out and quietly walked past the unconscious Night and Leaf. He started running quietly because even though Night and Leaf were down he was still outnumbered 5 to 1 which included a hawk and he certainly didn't want to face that.

Now he realised the dump entrance was not very far but he still had to go past the plane where the others were. He started walking quietly but quickly and he soon saw the plane looming up nearby and he could hear some ruckus coming from the other cats. There was a big hill of dump nearby and he quietly started walking behind it and he heard some conversation coming across the air to him.

He recognised Norbert's voice saying 'Oh! You should have seen his face when I threatened to cut off one of his claws but instead I gave him some scratches and that was enough for today'.

He heard Flame's voice saying 'Yes and also we got some very good loot today and how much longer shall we be in Paris?'

'A few more days and here is your sardine payment' answered Stryker from inside.

Simon heard purrs of delight and he heard the cats tucking in and he also continued to move forward when suddenly he lost his balance and fell against the heap which wobbled and collapsed making a tremendous noise. He heard the cats inside pause and say 'Hey! What was that?" and without giving a second thought Simon started running.

He heard the door open and Norbert shouting 'Hey! The prisoner is escaping."

Simon continued to run faster and he could hear the cats giving chase. He didn't look back and ran off in another direction to try and throw them off track. He risked a quick glance behind and saw only Snow, Flame and Shorty but no sign of Norbert or Stryker.

He thought that they must probably be coming from another direction as he veered off and scuttled among some junk and hid behind one, panting. There was silence for two three minutes when he heard some footsteps coming close to him and slowly peeking out he saw Shorty coming his way looking left and right for him.

He silently unsheathed his claws and held his breath as Shorty came closer and was nearly next to him when he suddenly leaped on Shorty and held him down and clawed his pelt as Shorty wriggled under him. He held him tight, pulled him upwards and threw him into a junk pile which caused a tiny avalanche and after it cleared Shorty was lying unconscious and half buried in the pile. Simon quickly ran from there.

Keeping his ears open for any sign of the others, he ran towards the dump entrance. He was getting closer as he saw the entrance come into view when suddenly something crashed into his side which sent him spinning down a slope and rolling him farther away from the entrance.

Before he could get up he felt something pin him down and he heard Snow's voice saying 'Here! I got him!'

Then he heard Flame coming and stood in front of him and snarled, 'Thought you could escape? Well you thought wrong cause you are not going anywhere'.

Simon then suddenly flipped over onto his belly which even though was dangerous was still effective as Snow went 'Huff!' and his weight was off him. He went staggering and was trying to regain his balance as Flame suddenly leaped at Simon, but Simon caught hold of him and sent him crashing into Snow.

He started running. He looked back and saw Flame coming for him again but his foot suddenly got stuck in a hole and Snow went to help him but the ground beneath them gave away a little and they both got stuck in the hole and were wriggling and thrashing about which only made them sink deeper.

Simon quickly ran up the slope and started running towards the entrance again and as he was getting closer he started thinking about freedom when suddenly a shadow passed over the moon. He glanced up and Stryker flying upwards with Norbert on his back. Stryker suddenly screeched and flew down at him with talons outstretched.

Thinking fast Simon went completely flat on the ground as Stryker's talons flew by where his head had been a minute before and he flew up and prepared for another strike.

He flew down again with Norbert on his back and Simon knew he had to end this battle fast and quickly. Glancing around, he saw some sand nearby. Taking some in a paw he looked up as Stryker flew down like a jet and then he suddenly threw the sand into Stryker's eyes.

Stryker howled loudly and veered off course with Norbert looking surprised and they crashed into the top of a junk pile and went spinning and sliding out of sight.

Simon now suddenly saw the entrance very close and he was nearly there when he heard some footsteps behind him and looked around and saw Norbert looking ragged but still strong. He panted and said, 'You knocked out Stryker but I wasn't so easy!'

Just as he finished Simon started running for the gate again with a very fast pace. 'Wait!' snarled Norbert very loudly and sprinted quickly and managed to grab hold of Simon's tail just as he reached the entrance. Simon suddenly swiped at his face and Norbert felt blood on his face as Simon's claws left a deep mark.

Norbert howled in pain and bit hard into Simon's shoulder but let go of his tail in the process. He grabbed hold of him and pinned him down. He had not pinned him for more than a few seconds when he felt Simon kick on his stomach which made Norbert stagger and released him. Simon quickly bolted and he would have escaped had Stryker not suddenly flown from his side and knocked him away and held him down tight.

Flame and Snow suddenly appeared then, evidently free and they reached Simon and glared at him. Shorty closely followed by a bloody Night and Leaf arrived then and snarled at Simon.

Norbert suddenly growled at Simon 'Well you filthy scum thought you could escape could you? But no! Night and Leaf take him back and attach the special lock to his bonds this time!'

Then he turned to the others and said, 'All of you should be ashamed of yourselves. Except you Stryker. For not being able to catch him. Cleaning for all of you tomorrow!'

Chapter 10

The Maze Challenge

The next day Nick and Francis trudged out of the alley and started looking around for Simon. They talked a little as they went.

'So, you were in this place and this Norbert came to you and you beat him and weren't angry anymore. Then you learnt you have got something that you don't know what yet!' said Nick to Simon as they trudged on.

'Yes but it was still nice killing that Norbert even though he wasn't the real one' said Francis. 'Look there's a cat over there! Let us see if she knows anything'.

They went over to the cat and Nick asked 'Have you seen any cats and a hawk?'

The cat turned around and asked 'Quoi?'

'I don't think you understood us, have you seen some cats and a hawk?' repeated Nick.

The cat answered 'Oh oui, j'ai vu beaucoup de chat et quelques faucons'.

'I don't think she understands us and we don't understand her' said Nick and he sighed and along with Francis went away.

'I wish we had some wishing power so we could find out where they have kept Simon' said Francis.

'Yes! Or someone from whom we could find out information from' said Nick.

'Did I hear you two say that you wanted to find out someone who could find out anything?' called out a familiar voice and a small figure scuttled out of the darkness.

'Ettie!' cried Francis in surprise.

'What are you doing here?' asked Nick.

'I was passing by and I heard you talking and recognised you. Where is Simon?' asked Ettie.

'Uh....' said Francis. 'I can't say exactly but he is definitely somewhere in this city' he finished.

'Oh! Well I have the answer to your problem. Follow me!' cried Ettie and started scuttling and Francis and Nick followed her.

She led them deep into the city and soon they came to the poorer parts of Paris but she continued scuttling and Nick and Francis continued to follow her. Soon Ettie paused beside a broken doorway leading down to some stairs underground.

'There! Go in' said Ettie.

'But who is down there?' asked Francis.

'There is a dog there who can tell you anything but in order to reach her you must go through a maze that has many traps' Ettie informed them.

'Okay' said Francis though he was still a bit unsure about this whole thing.

'I will wait here and if you do get caught by a trap, don't worry, they will put you back at the starting. But that is the end of it. Which means you can't go back in there ever again, so be careful!' warned Ettie.

'Uh, sure' said Nick and he and Francis went down and into the underground cavern and tried to be as brave as possible unaware of the challenge that they were going to face.

They emerged into a small underground room where a cat sat behind a stone desk. 'Are you here to see the famous know-it-all dog?' he asked.

'Yes' replied Nick. 'Where is the maze?'

'Through that tunnel' said the cat pointing with his paw to a tunnel leading off the room.

Nick and Francis took a deep breath and started into the tunnel.

It became a little dark but there was still enough light to see and soon they reached a sign that said 'Welcome to the maze.' They walked ahead and were soon into the maze and ran into a roadblock immediately. The path which they were on split off into two other parts, one going left and one going right.

'Which way should we go?' asked Nick.

'I'd say left' said Francis and that was the direction in which they went. Soon they reached another fork but this time with three parts.

'I'd say right this time' said Francis.

'No left!' cried Nick.

'Right' said Francis firmly.

'Left' cried Nick.

'I suppose there is only one way to settle this' said Francis and he looked around and spotted a rock which was different on both sides and said, 'I will flip this rock and if I get this side we will go right and if this side then left.'

'Fine by me' said Nick.

Francis picked up the rock in his mouth and flung it into the air. The rock kept spinning and changing side as it started to come down but when it finally hit the ground, the tip of the rock got buried in the sand over there and stood straight.

'What does this mean?' asked Francis.

'I suppose it means we have to take the centre path instead' said Nick and he and Francis walked into the centre path.

In the tunnel Nick suddenly said, 'Wait isn't it odd, we haven't come across any traps yet?'

As he said this, suddenly there was a rumbling in the ground in front of them and Francis and Nick quickly backed off as the ground in front of them opened up into a big hole and the two of them had barely escaped.

'Woah that was a close one!' cried Nick.

'Yes, look the hole isn't sealing itself up so I suppose any traps that have been activated, stay that way until we finish the course!' said Francis.

The only thing left to do now was to go back and try another way. They went back to the tunnel where the three fork ways were there. 'Let us do another toss this time' said Francis and he picked out another uneven rock and tossed it into the air and it settled on the ground

'There! According to this, we have to go right' said Nick.

They went into the right tunnel and after some walking they were approaching another fork but this time with five different directions but before that as they got closer to it Nick's paw pressed onto the ground. It was actually a switch. Suddenly there was a deep rumbling behind them and a huge boulder came towards them from back and started rolling at a fast speed towards them.

'Run!' cried Nick and he and Francis ran quickly ahead with the boulder right behind on their tails, literally and as they reached thee fork they both automatically decided to take the leftmost path as the boulder behind them rolled and disappeared into the centre tunnel.

'Phew! That was close,' said Francis.

'Yes but if we had our blasters with us we could have just blasted that rock into smithereens instead of running away' said Nick.

'Which reminds me that we haven't been using our gadgets much. So next time we should definitely take our gadgets with us when we go looking for Simon' said Francis.

'Yes, you are right' said Nick. 'Let us continue on this path now.' So they continued walking on it for a few minutes when they reached another fork but this one with a sign on it.

It said 'You are close! Only three more right choices will let you reach the final stage. But beware! One wrong choice will let you fall into a trap which will cast you out'

'Huh!' said Francis. 'So we are close to the final stage but we have three choices of direction'.

'Yes! So in this case, let me use my ears and nose' said Nick and he listened and he detected a faint trace of air from the left path and said. 'I can detect some air from the left path let us go there'

So they both veered into the left path. After a few minutes of walking they emerged in a large cavern with five paths.

'Oh no! Which path shall we take?' cried Francis.

'Don't worry! My nose can detect some air from the right path we shall take that' said Nick.

'Wait! My cat senses say that there is something wrong with that path' said Francis.

'I think they are wrong. This path is completely fine' said Nick and he went inside with Francis hesitantly following him. But they hadn't walked for more than a minute when a deep rumbling came in front of them and a big log of giant wood came rolling at a fast pace towards them and it filled up the entire cave.

'Ah! Run' cried Nick and he and Francis went running with the giant wood right behind them and as they neared the tunnel which led back to the fork, Nick cried 'I am sorry I should have listened to your cat senses!'

'Its okay,' said Francis. 'They now say that the centre path is the correct path!' He continued and they reached back into the fork tavern. They both quickly veered off into the centre path and the big roll of wood crashed against the entrance and stood where it was blocking the entrance to the tunnel.

As for Nick and Francis, they hurried down the tunnel they had chosen and soon emerged into an even larger cavern. They paused and were catching their breath. After a minute they looked around and saw that this was definitely the last cavern because there were at least ten paths to choose from and they all looked exactly the same.

'What do we do?' asked Nick and he looked at Francis and saw that he was breathing heavily.

Francis cried out 'I can't take this anymore!' and he quickly charged down one path with Nick quickly running after him but as they reached the end, they emerged into a tiny cave with three holes each sealed with a different colour cloth.

In front of them was another sign board which said 'Congratulations! You have reached the final stage. Decipher the riddle below and choose the colour cloth which is the answer.

It is a colour of a rainbow hue

And it is one of a fruit

It is friends with blue

And it is the colour of the king of fruits'

Nick looked up and saw the colour cloths of purple, red and green and said, 'Okay, so the correct answer is a rainbow colour so from these three only red and green are rainbow colours. Then the next line says it is a fruit colour but again red, green and purple all come in the category. So the line after that says it is friends with blue.

I know that red, green and blue are primary colours but red and green both come there so again it is not helpful. Finally the last line says it is the colour of the king of fruits but the king of fruits is a mango and a mango is yellow'.

'Hmm' said Francis and then he said, 'Wait I know that a mango is raw and when it is that it is green and not yellow so we have to take the path from the green cloth path'.

'Of course! Good thinking' complimented Nick and he went over and moved the green cloth. There was a slide behind it and they both slid down it and emerged in front of a door. Taking a deep breath they opened it and saw a large room with a desk on the end with a crystal ball on it and behind it sat a she-dog.

'Hello and congratulations on clearing the maze. I am Brownie and what can I do?' said the she-dog.

'I am Francis and this is Nick. His cousin has been catnapped by a couple of cats so can you find out where they are?' asked Francis.

'Of course' said Brownie and she closed her eyes and moved her paws around her ball for a few seconds. Then she opened her eyes and said 'I know where they are. In the sewers of Paris'.

'Thank you' cried Francis overjoyed as Brownie pressed a button on her desk and a tunnel opened up into the wall. 'This path shall take you directly towards the entrance'

Nick and Francis quickly bolted on. In a minute they were back in the reception and they quickly bounded up the stairs. They emerged back into the sunlight and Ettie opened her mouth to say something but Nick quickly said, 'Thank you Ettie for bringing us here, good bye!'

Then he and Francis ran towards their base to get their gadgets and then go into the sewer.

Chapter 11

Into The Sewer

'Well, here's an entrance to the sewer' said Nick as he and Francis stopped in front of a drain with a lid on top of it.

He and Francis worked together and opened the lid and saw a ladder leading off into the darkness.

'Simon, here we come!' said Francis and he and Nick started climbing off into the darkness and soon reached solid ground.

'Start the lights' said Nick and he and Francis took out a square box looking thing from their bag and switched it on illuminating the sewers. They immediately saw that it wasn't a good place as all around them were walls which were all dirty and looked as if they hadn't been scrubbed in a long time. The worst thing was the river like thing in the middle which stank so badly that Nick and Francis had to cover up their noses.

'Ugh! This place is horrible I can't believe that those criminal cats chose such a bad place to hide' said Francis.

'Yes but they must have been really desperate that they chose such a hiding place' said Nick. 'Let us look around for them.' He set off down a path with Francis following him and after a few minutes they came at an inter section with the path setting off into three different ways.

They wanted to go through the centre path and for that they had to jump over the stinky water so they ran forward and jumped over the water and landed on the path ahead.

'Blech! This place makes me feel like throwing up,' said Francis 'and what would have happened if we had landed in that water? We would stink so badly!'

'I agree with you' said Nick as they set off again while taking out their blasters and looking around warily in case something decided to come out: the cats or anything else. There was silence for another two minutes as they continued walking and then suddenly they heard a chittering sound coming from somewhere near them. They went close to it and three rats nearby were chattering among themselves.

'I didn't know rats were living here,' said Nick.

'I am not as surprised as you as this place is pretty stinky! So I am not surprised that they are living here as this place is so bad' replied Francis.

'Let us go' said Nick and he and Francis turned to walk away.

Suddenly the rats heard them and shouted 'Hey! What are you doing down here?'

Francis turned around and said, 'Well....'

But he was interrupted by a rat who said 'They must be from The Agency'.

Then another shouted 'Let us get them!' and they started advancing forward.

Nick then said, 'Hold on a minute! You are three rats against a cat and a dog don't you think the odds are against you'.

The third rat smirked and called out loudly 'The Agency is invading! Everybody come quickly!' Many red eyes glinted in the darkness and many rats came pouring out of the darkness and stood by the three rats.

One of the rats then said, 'I think the odds are now against you' and he bellowed 'All of you get them!'

All of the rats started running after Nick and Francis who immediately turned around and started running very quickly with the rats in hot pursuit. Then suddenly they saw they were nearing a gap too big to jump. They quickly pulled out a gadget from their bags and immediately pressed a button on it and it carried them up into the air. They were careful not to hit the ceiling and they sailed over the water and landed on the other side of the gap and turned back to the rats who had stopped on the other side and Nick called out 'Ha! You can't swim'.

A rat bigger than the rest and who must be the leader came forward and said, 'Rats! Form a rat bridge!' Four rats came forward and stood where they were and four others came and stood on their shoulders and four others came and stood on their shoulders and so on until they reached up to the ceiling and they started coming down and blam! A neat bridges of rats was formed and the remaining rats started crossing towards the other side!

Francis said, 'I think we should run now!'

Nick nodded and they immediately turned and started running again and behind them the rat bridge used all its strength so that the entire bridge was standing in a straight position up in the air and then they gently came down the other side. Then all the rats deformed and helped the four last rats who were clinging tightly to the wall and started running after Nick and Francis again.

'Quickly, use a gadget to stall them!' cried Francis and Nick took out a gun like thing and fired it in front of the rats and at first it looked like everything was normal but when the rats reached the spot where the gun had fired, they bounced into something and bounced back and fell on the ground and all the rats came to a stop.

The leader came and touched with his paw and for a brief moment a small bubble emerged in a space and then it disappeared again and Nick said, 'That will stay there for an hour, see you never!'

Then he and Francis started running again. After a few minutes of running and jumping in the sewer they stopped to catch their breath.

'Phew!' said Nick. 'Those guys seemed to talk in such a way that we were bad guys!'

Francis replied, 'They must have been talking about some other agency. I have never known of our agency to cause any trouble for them'.

'At least we are safe now' said Nick but as he said that there was the sound of footsteps and the rats appeared around a corner.

The lead rat said smiling, 'We know all the best ways in this sewer. Now rats form a rat carriage'. As he said this all the rats joined together again and soon a rat horse was formed and there were four rats on each foot and two ropes of rats was attached to a carriage of the rats with two rats holding the tails of the last rats of the rat string and the leader sat in the carriage upon his minions.

'Move it!' he cried and all the rats started moving after Nick and Francis who started running again with the rats on the horse feet the strongest rats and with the heavy weight on their back they started running. Soon the chase continued and Nick and Francis put on a burst of speed and slowly ran ahead of the rats.

The rat leader cried, 'Rats! Deform' and immediately all the rats deformed and were running normally with the rat leader in front who cried, 'Now for our fastest form so form of rat train!' and immediately the rats got into action.

Soon the train was formed. It consisted of all the rats as the main body and a few formed the chimney and as for the wheels they consisted of the rats who were the best at somersaulting and whose hard heads weren't bothered by the sewer floor. They were in a continuous circle and they all started rotating at the same time with each rat hitting the hard floor. This was definitely the fastest form as the rats were quickly gaining on Nick and Francis and the rat leader who sat leaning against the chimney shouted 'Almost there!' as the train sped up.

Nick and Francis ran faster than they had ever run and turned a corner and saw a dog and a cat up ahead looking around.

They both shouted 'Help us!' but they were going too fast to stop and Nick and Francis both crashed into them which is when they realised that they were over a long drop in the sewer. All four of them fell down and hit the ground very hard and lost consciousness.

Nick struggled and started waking up but found he could not move and his head was sore. He opened his eyes and saw Francis lying a few feet ahead of him also waking up. He couldn't tell how long they had been out and he saw no sign of the other cat and dog.

Then he realised that they were surrounded by rats and he gathered all his strength and managed to barely get up and Francis behind him was similar. Then he realised that they both didn't have their gadget pouches.

The rat leader stepped forward and said, 'At last you have woken up. Don't worry. We won't harm you.'

Nick then asked 'What has happened? How long have I been out?'

The leader said, 'Take it easy, I will explain'.

After Nick edged closer, Francis did the same.

The rat leader started talking, 'We first thought you were from the Agency which consists of dogs and cats who plan to make to make our sewer part of their base. Naturally we refused. We have been at war with them for it with our strength in numbers. After you and the others fell down and lost consciousness we saw that on the other dog and cat there were I.D. badges and we couldn't find yours anywhere. So we decided that you weren't part of it but the other two were. They were scouts planning the best way of attack and they were also unconscious but a few hours ago they also woke up and are now prisoners. We took away your bags for safekeeping and have been keeping an eye on you for the past three days and that's it'.

'Wait we have been knocked out for three days!?' cried Francis.

'Whoa! Relax this is a hard drop and your heads aren't very hard' said the rat leader.

'Yes he is right, Francis relax!' said Nick and Francis immediately calmed down.

'What were you two doing in the sewer anyway?' asked the leader.

Nick said, 'We are on a mission to catch a couple of criminal cats and they are hiding in your sewer with my friend's cousin catnapped by them'.

The rat leader looked puzzled and said, 'You must have got the wrong address. We patrol our sewer every day and no cat is down here, I am sure of it'.

Francis turned to Nick and said, 'If the cats are not here that means...'

'Brownie lied to us!' finished Nick looking mad and said to the rat leader 'We need your help will you help us?'

The rat leader said, 'After you caught those two scouts, anything!'

'Good! We need around fifty of your best fighters and the closest exit to a broken building where a soothsayer dog is' said Nick.

'Yes it is close by' said the leader and he gave a sharp cry and fifty rats came forward with Nick and Francis's gadget bags.

Francis said, 'I understand what you are doing and I will support you with this' and he turned to the leader and said, 'Come on let's go' and taking his bag he and Nick and the others started marching and after a few minutes came to a spot where there was a ladder stretching up.

He climbed up it and popped open the hole and peeked his head out and saw it was nearly night and he was a few streets away from the building. He moved out and Nick and the rats followed and they marched down the stairs and emerged back into the reception room.

The cat who sat there looked over his desk and said, 'What's going on?' and Nick whispered to the rat leader.

The leader shouted 'Rats, grab him and take him to our jail!' and twenty rats leaped and grabbed the cat and held him down who tried to struggle but the rats held him tight and carried him off.

Nick pressed a button on the cat's desk and the tunnel to Brownie's room opened and they all marched in. They soon emerged into the room where Brownie was sitting in her spot and upon seeing them she said, 'You two thank goodness! I made a mistake!'

But she was cut off by Francis who said 'You certainly did!'

Then the remaining thirty rats leaped on her and soon she was being carried off as she went she shouted 'Wait! Your cousin is being held captive in the dump of Paris!'

But Nick just said, 'Oh! Shut up we are not listening to you anymore' as he rolled her crystal ball of the desk where it shattered on the floor.

Soon Nick and Francis and the leader climbed out and the leader said 'I must go now as well. Farewell!'

But Nick said 'Wait' and he took out a powerful looking blaster and gave it to the leader who just managed to hold it and he explained, 'This blaster when you hit a soldier of an army, the entire army will go to sleep for twenty four hours. We are from the Detective and Spy House Agency and we would like to form a friendship with your clan'.

The leader nodded and said, 'Thank you' and he walked back into the sewer as Francis called out 'Wait, we don't know your name!'

The leader said 'It's Shady' and then he was gone.

Nick and Francis also walked back and Francis said, 'Well that's the last time I trust people who know everything.'

Nick nodded and said, 'Me too' as they both walked off into the night.

Chapter 12

A Stalking Trail

The next evening Nick and Francis sat down to some supper after a fruitless day of searching for Simon. They nibbled at the remaining food from the dumpster which consisted of some apple cores and a remaining fish skin.

'It has been nearly a week since we have arrived in Paris and all we have succeeded in, is not catching the cats and getting Simon catnapped' said Francis gloomily.

Nick nodded and said, 'You are right'.

Then he stood up and said, 'Wait I have got an idea, we will go after them'

'What! Are you an idiot?! Those cats clearly said that if we go after them at night they will do something bad to Simon' said Francis.

'No not exactly go after them. We will quietly follow them after they steal and they will lead us right back to their base when we will strike with our gadgets and take back Simon, capture those cats and their employer and take them back to jail' explained Nick.

'I am still unsure about this but I will go with you on this plan' said Francis and they started to get ready for their new plan at night.

That night in the shadows two figures lingered and quietly ran from one street to another while keeping their blasters close and hidden. These figures as you must have guessed were none other than Nick and Francis themselves. Sticking together and finding the cats in Paris while hiding was of course no easy job.

They crossed a few more streets stealthily and stood in the shadow of a tall apartment building. 'I have a hunch that Norbert and the other cats will strike here tonight' said Nick.

'How can you be sure?' asked Francis.

'I have heard there is plenty of wealth in the top floor so they will definitely strike here' answered Nick.

'I hope you are right. Let us wait in those barrels' said Francis and so they got inside them and waited and waited. After a long time they heard some scuffling on the roof ahead of them and Norbert's head peeked over and he swung a grappling hook.

It landed on the roof above them and he swung and gracefully landed on the roof. Snow and Flame's head then peeked over next and then they swung two grappling hooks and when they were attached they also started to swing. However when they had almost reached, they suddenly swung into each other and went crashing and landed hard on the roof.

Norbert muttered something under his breath and went over and gave Snow and Flame a hard whack on the head and they immediately stood up straight. Behind them Nick and Francis saw Night, Leaf and Shorty, the other three cats, also throw grappling hooks and they swung and their success was better than Snow and Flame's but not as good as Norbert's.

They all scuttled after him and soon they were out of sight. 'Let us go and capture them now' said Francis as he started to climb out of the barrel.

'Wait! Remember we are only supposed to follow them back to their lair and not engage until they show us their hideout' reminded Nick.

'It's so frustrating! They are so close to us and we have to stay hidden in this barrel and wait for them' muttered Francis but he obeyed and soon they heard the cats coming back out with bags slung over their shoulders.

Then the six cats leaped onto another rooftop and they continued to jump despite their heavy load.

'Hurry! They are going out of sight' said Nick and he and Francis quickly leapt out of the barrels and started running after the cats while making sure to stay hidden in the shadows. They moved with quick precise movements always keeping the robber cats two rooftops ahead of them.

Just then they saw Flame stopping and he whispered something to Snow who whispered it to Norbert and then all six of them turned to look at where Nick and Francis were hiding. Night decided to go and investigate and he slid down a drainpipe and came onto the ground where he started walking towards where Nick and Francis were.

Both of them quickly looked around for somewhere to hide and saw a trash can. As much as they would regret it, it was a good hiding spot as it would hide their scent and nobody would ever suspect they would hide there.

As quick as lightning they quickly went inside the trash can and had barely settled when they saw Night emerge to where they had been. He looked around for some time but didn't find any scent or anything so he trudged back to his friends and as soon as the cats had set off Nick and Francis clambered out of the trash.

'I am never getting into a trash can as long as I live!' declared Francis trying to get the trash smell off him.

'Same here' said Nick doing the same. Then after a minute they started looking frantically around for the cats. After a minute when they had given up hope of finding them, they heard some bags being dragged around in the building in front of them.

Quickly looking around, they saw some crates and lay low behind them just as Norbert followed by Snow and Flame poked their heads out of the window carrying a few more sacks.

'Oh no! They are going to jump down and they might see us' whispered Francis.

'Come on, let us hide inside the crate' whispered Nick.

Keeping silent, they quietly opened the lid and crept out of sight inside the crate. Just as they shut the lid, they heard Norbert land with a thump next to them followed by a few more thumps as the other cats landed next to them and heard them walking off.

'Okay now let us go after them again' said Francis but just then they felt the crate being lifted up and heard some human voices outside. They felt the crate being loaded on the back of what felt like a coach and felt another crate being put on top of them and more around them and then they heard the coach being put in motion.

'Quickly we have to get out!' cried Nick and then they pushed against the lid but because of the other crate on top of it they couldn't remove it and nothing seemed to work.

'Wait, move as far as you can' said Francis suddenly.

'What are you going to do?' asked Nick.

'Just watch' said Francis and he fired a big beam from the blaster.

BLAM! It was so loud they both were nearly deafened but the crate was almost destroyed now and the carriage was slowing down and Nick and Francis quickly jumped off and scuttled into the darkness.

'That was an idiotic thing to do Francis!' yelled Nick when they had gone a considerable distance. 'You could have gotten us either killed or blown up the coach which are both equally bad!' '

I know I am sorry but don't worry I assure you it won't happen again' said Francis.

With great restraint Nick said 'Fine but don't you realize we won't be able to find the cats now so there is nothing left except go back to the base'

'Oh no! I didn't realize that but we will definitely use this plan to catch them tomorrow night' said Francis.

But there wasn't to be a tomorrow night because that night when Nick and Francis were sleeping, Nick heard some scuffling on the rooftop and he woke up and saw a paper note coming down from there and a cat's tail just disappearing. He didn't follow because he knew that by the time he got there the cat would have gotten away.

He woke up Francis and told him what had happened.

'Well, read out what the note says' said Francis.

Nick opened the note and read out 'Dear Nick and Francis, tomorrow night we will do our grand robbery so we thought we will drop Simon off to you. Meet us at the Jardin des Tuilleries Garden at midnight sharp. Don't be late. Signed, Norbert'.

'Well what do you say Francis?' asked Nick.

'We are definitely going Nick, and he didn't say not to bring any gadgets so we are taking them too and my bowling balls' answered Francis.

'We are in this together' said Nick and Francis nodded and they stood at the night sky waiting patiently for the next night.

Chapter 13

A Grand Slam Robbery of Paris

The next night near eleven Nick and Francis started packing and getting ready for the task ahead of them.

'Right! It will take about an hour to reach there and we have asked for directions this morning so we will leave in a minute' said Francis putting his bowling balls in his gadget bag.

'Yes and don't worry we will get Simon back and catch those cats' said Nick.

They then looked around there base one last time because they had a feeling they wouldn't be here again and set off. It was a dark night, they walked and walked and soon after what felt like two hours instead of one, they reached the gate of the garden.

It was shut but they both threw a rope and hoisted themselves up and entered the

111

garden. Glancing around them they saw it was really big and expansive and there were many trees and flowers around them and there were also many pathways to walk on.

'Well here we are' said Nick.

'Yes what is the time anyway?' asked Francis.

'It is five minutes to twelve' answered Nick 'I wonder is there a specific spot we are supposed to meet them?'

'The letter only said to wait in the garden but no specific spot so I suppose we have to wait here' said Francis.

So they waited patiently for five minutes and another five and another five. It was ten minutes past twelve and nobody had still arrived.

'Where is everybody?' asked Nick getting bored.

'Same here' muttered Francis.

Just then a voice called out 'So my dear friends you have arrived' and a black cat stepped out of the shadows.

'You!' growled Francis and took out his blaster as did Nick.

'Now! Now put that down we don't want any uncomfortable violence now do we?'

said the cat and then said, 'I don't think we have been properly introduced, my name is Night and those two behind you are Leaf and Shorty.'

'What?' cried Nick and Francis at the same time and turned around to catch two mighty attack swipes.

Leaf leaped on Nick and put his hind leg beneath him and toppled him and Shorty slashed Francis's muzzle which made him reel and then gave a mighty scratch to his cheek and sent him toppling.

'There I told you no funny business! Now come follow me if you want to see your friend again' said Night as he calmly took away Nick and Simon's blasters and put them back in the bag before slinging them over his shoulders and added, 'Leaf and Shorty keep your eyes on them in case they do anything else'.

Then he calmly strutted towards another corner where another rope was there while behind him Leaf and Shorty put their claws behind Nick and Francis and pushed them forward.

'Why are you late anyway? You said you will come at midnight but you came ten minutes late' asked Nick .

'Oh! We fell asleep' answered Shorty.

'Yes don't we also feel tired after all our robberies?' said Leaf.

'No talking please and hurry up!' requested Night.

They walked in silence for a few minutes and then soon they emerged in front of a building. It wasn't just any building, it had a big wall surrounding it and inside was an open space occupied by a few pyramid shaped structures and behind them a huge building.

'Ah! The Louvre Museum' said Night and then he led them inside a building in front of the Louvre. They went to the back of the building and stepped on a wooden platform which had ropes on it from all four sides.

'Flame! My pal! Can you let us up?' called out Night and they heard Flame's voice reply, 'Yes, I am hoisting you up.'

Then the platform began to move upwards and they heard some grunting and panting from Flame as he pulled them up. They soon reached the top and stepped down from the platform and Flame bounded away from a pulley system and over to Snow who had emerged from behind a chimney.

Snow surveyed everything and said, 'Well it looks like we have you in our paws this time. Night has possession of your gadgets and your cousin is captured Francis, so don't try anything'.

'Where is he anyway? And for that matter where is Norbert and your employer?' demanded Francis.

'Oh! Don't worry they will be here soon oh! But there they are' said Snow and a big shadow passed above them and a big hawk landed on top of the chimney with Norbert sitting on the hawk.

'Greetings' said the hawk. 'I am Stryker and you two must be the Nick and Francis I have heard so much about so did you get our letter?'

'We wouldn't be here then would we?' growled Nick.

'Of course! Leaf is the best postal service cat isn't he?' said Norbert and Leaf smiled.

'Where is Simon?' demanded Francis.

'Oh! Here he is' said Norbert and then he got down from Stryker and reached out behind him and pushed a scraggy bundle of black fur ahead.

Simon didn't look like himself anymore. He had several scratches along his body and a few new scars. He was limping on one foot and one of his ears was badly torn.

'What have you done to him?' growled Francis.

'I just wanted some information of the Detective and Spy House Agency and to make him talk I had to make some scratches but he never said anything,' said Norbert calmly.

'Why you?!' growled Francis seething with rage.

'Any way this talking isn't getting us anywhere. Stryker here are their gadgets, keep a good eye on them and on Simon while we go and do our tenth and final robbery of Paris. Let us give our new introduction before we go' said Norbert and then they launched into their new motto.

Flame: A gang of robbers...

Snow: Born to be the best of them all

Night: There's me

Leaf: And me

Shorty: And me too

Norbert: Correct

Flame: A ginger tabby I am Flame

Snow: A white tortoiseshell I am Snow

Night: A black Abyssinian I am Night

Leaf: A sandy coloured with a green tinge Siberian I am Leaf

Shorty: And a small Sphynx cat I am Shorty

Norbert: And the leader a brown Persian I am Norbert

Stryker: And a deadly hawk I am Stryker

All: And now say hello to the new Team Cat!

'We don't have time for this!' growled Nick.

'Yeah! You're right!' said Shorty.

'Come on, let us go' ordered Norbert and they all went down the elevator and went back to the ground floor and they walked across the street and climbed over the walls and disappeared from sight.

'Stryker, can we please talk to Simon?' requested Francis.

'Norbert told me not to do that' reminded Stryker.

'He only told you to keep an eye on us and we aren't going anywhere' said Nick.

'Okay I suppose so but only for three minutes' said Stryker.

'Thank you!' said Francis.

Stryker let go of Simon and he walked as fast as he could over to them.

'It's so nice to see you again!' exclaimed Simon as they embraced each other.

'Don't worry Simon, we will free you from their clutches' whispered Nick.

'Where were you anyway?' asked Francis.

'The cats took me to their hideout which was in the dump of Paris' answered Simon.

'The dump!?' exclaimed Nick and Francis and started at each other and both of them thought 'Brownie had been right after all oh! If only they had listened to her at that time'

'What's wrong? What are you both thinking?' asked Simon after seeing the expression on their faces.

'Nothing' said Francis.

'Three minutes are up!' called Stryker and Simon reluctantly walked back.

A few minutes later there was a sound coming from the elevator and Norbert's voice came up, 'Stryker pull us up please' he said.

Stryker walked over there while still keeping hold of Simon and the two gadget bags and started to hoist the cats up and soon the elevator appeared and the cats got down. Nick and Francis noticed Snow and Flame carrying a huge painting which had a lady smiling on it and a good background behind it.

'Right Norbert, now you have finished your robbery so please give Simon back to us' requested Francis.

'Okay' said Norbert and Stryker let Simon go and Simon started to walk when Norbert said, 'Not' and Stryker grabbed Simon once again and held him close.

'What are you doing!?' cried Nick.

'As if we would give Simon back to you we are villains and we never keep our word' taunted Leaf.

Simon then suddenly bit Stryker's wing and Stryker hobbled but Simon quickly rushed forward while also taking the two gadget bags from Stryker.

'Night stop him!' ordered Norbert and Night bounded forward.

'Oh no, you don't' said Francis and he charged forward and gave Night a deep scratch on his cheek.

'Ah! It burns! It burns!' cried Night and stepped back allowing Simon to reach Nick and Francis.

'Don't be a coward of course it will burn!' growled Norbert 'No! It burns so badly it feels like my cheek is on fire oh! The agony' cried Night.

'That is your special power Francis!' cried Nick suddenly. 'Whenever you claw someone, it's like their wounds are on fire.'

'Really?' said Francis staring down at his claws.

'That doesn't help you. Stryker now!' cried Norbert and Stryker suddenly flew forward and grabbed the gadget bags back and was flying back when Nick grabbed his leg and while he was trying to shake him off, Francis's bowling balls came out of the bag and fell next to the chimney.

'Stryker, throw away the bags!' ordered Norbert and Stryker threw them and shook Nick off and flew back and landed with the rest of Team Cat.

'Well, it looks like you got Simon back but you aren't getting us without a fight' said Norbert and all the other cats including Night who had stopped wailing, unsheathed their claws and Snow and Flame dropped their painting and pushed it behind them and bared their teeth. Norbert then leaped on top of Stryker who rose and hovered a little above the ground.

'Simon can you fight?' asked Francis.

'I may have bad wounds but I can still fight' said Simon unsheathing his claws and so did Nick and Francis.

'Well we lost our gadgets so we are going to have to fight with bare teeth and claws' said Nick and bared his teeth as did Francis and Simon preparing for the battle ahead.

Chapter 14

A Fight and the Beginning of a Chase

The two sides stared at each other then Nick cried, 'Charge!'

Nick, Francis and Simon started running forward when Norbert cried, 'The Team Cat battle cry Mrraoow!' and they also charged forward and the two sides crashed into each other and the battle began.

Francis leaped for Shorty and gave him a very sharp slash across the stomach and Shorty cried, 'It's so hot! It's so hot!' and hearing his cries Night and Leaf bounded forward to help him but Francis swiped Night's ear and then quickly slid under him and gave a kick to his belly which sent him flying.

He then leaped on Leaf's back and using his same tactic, hooked his hind leg beneath Leaf's and toppled him and then sunk his teeth into his shoulder which made Leaf cry out badly in pain. Then he felt teeth sink in his shoulder and he was dragged off Leaf and he turned his head to see who it was and he saw it was Night who suddenly caught his muzzle with a vicious swipe.

The pain was searing but Francis wasn't giving these cats the satisfaction of seeing him in pain so he kept silent and he felt Night throw him forward and straight into Shorty's paws. Shorty held him tight and raked his ear and Night bounded forward and thinking fast, Francis used his hind paws and gauged Night's belly which was very bad for him. He then managed to sink his teeth a little into Shorty's shoulder which made his grip loosen a little.

Just as he was summoning the willpower to throw him off, he felt Leaf dig into his tail and Shorty tightened his grip then with their combined strength they threw him and sent him flying. As he was mid-air, Night leaped up and gave his cheek such a vicious blow that it changed his course and he crashed right into the chimney which knocked the breath out of him and he slid down, defeated.

In the meantime, Simon had attacked Flame and held him down tight and had sunk his teeth into his shoulder when he felt Flame give a very strong kick on his gut which made him release him and stagger back a little. Flame leaped for him and knocked out his feet from under him and thinking fast, Simon dropped onto Flame before he could escape and knocked the breath out of him and pinned him tight. He heard a yowl and looked back just in time to catch a mighty swipe from Snow which pushed him away from Flame and knocked him down. Before he could get up, Snow landed on top of him and sank his teeth into his stomach.

Simon hooked onto Snow's hind paws and then sent him tumbling and they both rolled across the rooftop and kept delivering blows to each other. They suddenly stopped at the edge of the rooftop with Simon on top of Snow and he clawed at Snow's belly while Snow writhed under him trying to break free. Flame suddenly leaped at Simon and dragged him off Snow who immediately leaped to his feet and hooked onto Simon's scruff and together they both threw him and sent him tumbling across the rooftop.

He came to a stop but before he could get up, Snow leaped on top of him and dug his teeth deep inside his back. Then he lifted him up a little and flung him and Simon hit the back of his head against the chimney and fell next to Francis, defeated.

Nick had leaped up at the hovering Stryker and hooked onto his belly and dug his teeth deep inside Stryker's belly, who then let out a sharp cry and he felt wings going on batting at him and eventually they knocked him away and he fell to the ground. Stryker flew over him and Nick saw Norbert on his back and quickly leaped up and knocked Norbert off Stryker and they both fell to the ground.

Norbert found his feet first and leaped at Nick and sunk his teeth deep into his side and Nick suddenly bit into Norbert's ear who caught his stomach with a vicious kick and made Nick lose his grip. Nick stepped back and started to charge forward when he felt strong claws hook tightly onto his shoulders and felt himself lifted up into the air by Stryker.

He struck out with his hind paws but Stryker kept his grip and suddenly began to fly higher and then started spinning the loop-da-loop and Nick felt himself buffeted by the sheer wind and his vision swam in his eyes. After about seven of these Stryker suddenly let go of Nick who flew straight like a missile downwards and with a big thud got his face slammed by the chimney and he slid down in that position and landed between Simon and Francis also defeated.

Simon weakly got to his feet and looked at the rest of Team Cat closing in and said, 'Oh no! We are outnumbered, what do we do?' and Nick lifted up and got to his feet.

His face was completely bruised and both his eyes were black and he spat out a tooth and said, 'I don't know'.

Francis then staggered to his feet and said, 'There is only one thing we can do,' and he reached for the bowling balls box next to the chimney and slashed it open. He took out one ball and said, 'Bowling anyone?' and then he aimed for Leaf and threw it and it slammed Leaf right in the face!

'Okay' said Nick and Simon and they also took out two other bowling balls and threw them at Night and Shorty and they managed to avoid them hitting their faces but they didn't manage to avoid it hitting, their, well, it couldn't be said where.

As a hint, Night and Shorty were hit on the part of the body where it hurt the most when somebody hits you there.

'Come on!' yelled all three of them and each one picked up one of the three remaining bowling balls and charged forward with them.

'Snow and Flame, take care of them!' yelled Norbert frantically and the two of them charged forward yelling which was silenced when Nick and Simon threw their balls and it the two SMACK! In the face.

'This is for hurting Simon, Norbert!' yelled Francis and he threw his bowling ball at Norbert which missed him by about ten inches.

'Ha! You missed!' taunted Norbert.

'I don't think so' said Francis smiling as the bowling ball continued to fly forward and it hit the still hovering Stryker right in the belly and he angrily kicked it right up into the air and it sailed high up and shot down and crashed hard onto Norbert's head which made him stagger.

'Now let the battle continue!' yelled Nick and the three of them picked up two bowling balls each and charged forward. Nick charged straight at Snow and Flame who unsheathed their claws again and charged forward at him.

Nick waited until they were close enough and then jumped up in the air with the two balls and brought one down on Snow's head and the other on Flame's head. This made the two of them lose their footing and their cheeks touched each other for a brief moment. Seizing the opportunity, Nick bashed the two bowling balls on their other cheek at the same time, which made the two completely senseless.

They walked around dizzily and Nick continued to hit the two balls on the either one's head or on their face and then he smacked the bowling balls on their jaws which made them fly up in the air a little. Then Nick threw the bowling balls on their stomachs which sent flying even further and they landed side by side but that last shot had taken them out of the fight.

Simon had turned his attention on Night and Leaf who cowardly backed away while trembling at the same time and Simon boldly charged forward and hit the two balls on either one's snout which made both reel. He then bashed the bowling balls on their necks and then straight on their jaws which made them lift their forepaws and then Simon aimed the balls at their gut and sent them right up. Finally, he threw the balls at their faces while they were still airborne and they both landed on top of Snow and Flame.

As for Francis, he had attacked Norbert and Shorty.

Norbert shouted at Shorty 'Go, take care of him and save me!'

Shorty leaped forward in the air and flew straight at Francis with his head outstretched and yelled 'Rock butt!' but Francis calmly hit his head with one ball when he was close and with the other he hit his jaw and sent him flying and made him also land in the pile with the other cats.

Norbert charged forward with his claws outstretched and Francis calmly ducked under his attack and then shot up and smashed both the balls into Norbert's face at the same time. Then without giving Norbert a chance to recover, Francis kept smashing the balls one after the other into Norbert's face which pushed him back and then hit both the balls on his jaw and sent him also flying and crash landing in the pile on top of the others.

'Good job Francis!' complimented Nick as he walked over with Simon and they both had collected their bowling balls.

'Yeah! We won!' cried Simon.

'Aren't you forgetting someone?' asked a familiar voice and all three turned to see Stryker hovering at a high spot and nobody could expect their bowing ball to hit him at such height.

'Hah! Let us see you hit your legendary balls at me at this height' called Stryker

'What do we do? He is right, we can't hit him from here' said Nick.

'I think it is time to use the trick we performed at the Agency last week along with the balls' said Simon and Francis and Nick nodded.

Nick and Simon leaped up on the chimney where Simon jumped on top of Nick and he held out his two balls as did Nick. Francis then started running forward with his two balls and jumped up on the chimney and he picked up Nick's balls with his hind legs and then landed on top of Nick and immediately jumped up at Simon and propped his bowling balls against his sides and then jumped off Simon's back too and then flew right up in the air and when he was at his highest point, he started spinning around and threw the balls one by one up at the astonished Stryker who was so astonished that he didn't have time to dodge and one by one the balls started to hit him.

The first one hit him right in the face, the second in his gut, the third and fourth at the exact spot where the wings connected to his body, the fifth on his neck and the sixth right in the jaw. This attack was too much for him and he fell back to Earth and landed on the six cats who were starting to get up and knocked them down again.

Francis also landed next to the chimney and collected each bowling ball as they fell and put them back in the box and Nick and Simon also leaped down from the chimney. Francis picked up his box and he along with Nick and Simon walked over to the defeated Team Cat.

'Well Norbert, you have lost! So surrender and go to jail along with your friends' said Nick.

'Never!' rasped Norbert as he along with the others got to their feet. 'You may have beaten us but you won't catch us' he panted.

Then with lightning speed, Stryker flew up a little and Night and Leaf jumped up and he caught them in his claws. Shorty jumped up and hooked his claws into Stryker's side and

Norbert leaped for his spot on Stryker's back and as for Snow and Flame they held up the painting and shouted, 'Here is the Mona Lisa! Boss' and they threw up the painting to Norbert who caught it and then they leaped up as well at the uppermost part of Stryker's legs.

'Quickly to the elevator!' shouted Nick and they ran forward.

But Norbert said, 'I don't think so' and Stryker flew towards the elevator and in a few seconds, he cut away all four wires and the elevator tumbled down and smashed below.

'See you never!' taunted the cats as Stryker started to fly away.

'Team Cat, taste this!' yelled Francis and he threw the bowling box and it hit Stryker right in the head and all the cats screamed as Stryker plummeted downward.

'Now jump on them' cried Francis and he jumped.

'What!?' cried Nick and Simon but they obeyed and jumped down next to Francis and they landed on Stryker and this made the plummeting faster. They soon crashed and Flame landed on his feet while the others landed awkwardly which is unlike cats and he said, 'Wow, I actually...' but he was interrupted by Francis who landed on top of him and knocked Flame down.

'Hey watch it!' he cried and manage to roll off Francis and the other cats got up and started running.

But Stryker said, 'Ouch! I dislocated my wing I can't fly' and ran with the others.

Francis ran after them down the street and as they were about to turn a corner, there was a whirring sound and a light came forward and it hit the starting of the street and separated Norbert, Snow and Flame from the others.

Francis turned around to see Nick carrying a big gun with Simon behind him carrying their gadget bags.

'Simon found these so I thought I would use this' said Nick.

'Stryker, they have us cornered but don't worry, I have a plan. You take the others back to the dump and take the plane and meet us at the top of the Eiffel Tower' said Norbert.

'Got it' said Stryker and he ushered the cats and they scuttled off along with the Mona Lisa which Stryker had.

'Come on! We also have to move' said Norbert.

But Nick said, 'Going somewhere?' and started to fire his gun.

'Oh no! You don't' said Norbert and from a pouch attached to his side he took out a wooden ninja star and threw it at Nick and it hit his paw and made his aim go awry.

'Let us move!' cried Norbert and he along with Snow and Flame started to run away.

Francis quickly pulled out the ninja star and asked 'What should we do?'

'We are also doing the same thing. Simon, you go back to our base and get our plane and meet us at the top of the Eiffel Tower and we will chase after them' said Nick urgently.

'Okay' said Simon and ran off.

'Come on Francis, we have some criminals to catch' said Nick.

Francis said, 'Yeah' and they both started running after them.

Chapter 15

The Chase Continues and has a Glorified Ending

As you may have read earlier, Francis had said he had wanted to visit the Eiffel Tower but a trip in which the cats had been caught not, when they were chasing them he barely had time to look around the tower.

That is what he was thinking as he and Nick ran chasing the three cats and the Eiffel Tower loomed closer and closer and the agents increased their speed and so did the three cats.

'Come on Nick! Let us use our blasters,' said Francis and Nick nodded and they both took out their blasters from their bags and started firing it at the three cats who screamed and dodged while the blasters hit targets behind them.

'Don't worry boss, I have a plan to delay them' whispered Snow in Norbert's ear and Norbert nodded.

Snow saw a barrel on the side and he scampered to it and then knocked it off and sent it in front of Nick and Francis who quickly raised their blasters and opened fire on the barrel and completely destroyed it.

'Is that all?' taunted Francis but he was silenced when Snow knocked five other barrels and sent them rolling at a fast pace and then quickly re-joined the others. They continued running while Nick and Francis were delayed for a few minutes as they managed to destroy each barrel before it crushed them.

They quickly charged forward and were catching up to the three cats but were still a distance away when they heard the cats arrive at the locked gate and heard Norbert say, 'Okay Flame, use your claws to open this lock,' and they heard Flame putting his claw in the lock as they came in sight of them.

Instead of picking the lock, Flame's claw broke and he cried out in pain and Norbert muttered under his breath and quickly inserted his claws and successfully picked the lock as the gate opened.

'Hurry! Before they catch us!' cried Norbert and they dashed off towards the stairs just as Nick and Francis also entered and dashed after them. The stairs were long and seemed to be never ending and by the time they had reached the third floor both the groups were panting but still kept going.

'Hey Snow do you remember how many stairs are there in the Eiffel Tower?' panted Flame.

'If I remember correctly there are 1,710 stairs' panted Snow.

'Stop chattering and run faster' ordered Norbert and they continued running up as did Nick and Francis who quickened their pace and charged faster.

'Francis, I have an idea' said Nick 'At the count of three we will both fire our force field guns in front of the cats and behind them and stop them from going further and we will arrest them then.'

'I don't know, it is risky. They might avoid it and we won't be able to chase them any further' answered Francis.

'Yes but our aim is too good, we will not miss' assured Nick and Francis sighed and nodded and they both continued running up and took out their force field guns.

Nick counted 'One, two three' and they both fired their guns at the same time and their aims fired in different places, Nick's fired right behind the cats and Francis's seemed that it would hit in front of the cats trapping them but at the last second the three cats jumped and dived as the force field formed behind them and the cats had successfully avoided the two force fields.

'Ha! Looks like your own plan backfired on you' taunted Norbert and he continued running along with Snow and Flame and Nick and Francis stopped short of the force fields.

'See Nick! I told you this might happen but you didn't listen so now, do you have any idea what to do?' yelled Francis.

Nick sighed and said, 'You were right, even people with very good aim can still miss and that is what happened, I am sorry but I don't have any idea what to do'.

Francis sighed and said, 'Well, I think we have only one option now. We have to launch our grappling hooks and then we can go up the tower and catch up to them'.

He then saw an opening and fired his grappling hook up there and swung and landed and after a moment so did Nick then they both fired them higher and again climbed up through them and just as they reached, they saw the three cats only one floor above them and so they quickly detached the hook and sped after them.

They ran even faster now and soon started gaining on them again and then started devising another plan to catch them. Francis got an idea and he whispered to Nick, 'Remember the latest technology at the Agency where there was a gun invented which could slow down a person and make him or her as slow as a tortoise for five minutes?'.

'Yes but what about it?' asked Nick.

'Well, I was asked to look after one and I brought it here' answered Francis and took the gun out of his bag.

Nick smiled and said, 'Nothing can go wrong with this idea'.

Francis fired two shots one after the other. One of them successfully hit the three cats and they started to slow down but the other bounced off a wall and rebounded and hit Nick and Francis.

'Except for that' muttered Nick.

They now engaged in a dramatically slow chase after the also dramatically slow moving cats.

'Stop!' said Nick very slowly and it made it sound more cavernous.

'Never!' came Norbert's equally cavernous voice.

'Nick, we have to think of another way' said Francis's cavernous voice.

'Boss, we have to move faster' said Flame and Snow cavernously together.

'Yes let us' said Norbert cavernously and they also started dramatically moving fast, well as fast as they could.

'We have to move faster too' said Nick cavernously.

Francis said, 'Agreed' cavernously.

Then the two groups started moving faster too and then after some time Francis's cavernous voice said, 'The effect should be wearing off in three... two... one...' and then they all returned to their normal speed and thankfully their normal voices as it was getting tiring writing "cavernous".

They continued chasing the cats up the stairs and Nick came up with another idea, 'Francis, there is also a gun which can make a person go very fast so let us zap ourselves and get ahead of these cats and arrest them'.

'Yes take out the gun and do zap ourselves' said Francis and Nick took out it out and raised it and prepared to fire but he suddenly stumbled and he accidently pressed the trigger and hit the three cats.

The cats immediately started charging up the stairs with superhuman speed or in this case supercat speed and Nick and Francis muttered under their breath, 'Here we go again' and zapped themselves and started charging up with supercat and superdog speed.

They ran as fast they could but the three cats also ran equally fast and so they zipped up the staircases and after a few minutes like the previous gun the effects wore off and they returned to their normal speed again and when they did so all of them were immediately very tired.

'Boss, I need some water' panted Flame.

'Me too' panted Snow.

Norbert panted and said, 'Me too, but there will be enough water on the plane so keep running as fast as you can'

'Oh! Did you know that we just ran up more than two thirds of the stairs and we are nearly at the top?' panted Snow.

As for Nick and Francis they kept running with their tongues out and after a minute or two Norbert turned back and asked, 'Hey! How about a time out for three minutes?'

'Yes' answered Nick and Francis at once too tired to argue or arrest them.

So the two groups stopped and stood catching their breath, their chests heaving and surprisingly though they were also just some distance from each other but neither of them moved.

Then Nick and Francis took out two water bottles and tossed one to Norbert almost forgetting that they were enemies and then each side drank some water from the bottle and stood and just whispered into their respective group member's ear.

After three minutes Nick said, 'Okay three minutes are up, let us continue the chase' and then they both started running after each other again.

Then Norbert turned back to look at them and said, 'You two have been trying some way to catch us and now it is our turn to attack'.

He took out three ninja stars from the pouch and threw it at Nick and Francis who immediately dodged to one side and narrowly avoided the stars.

'Nick don't worry, I have an idea!' said Francis as Norbert reached again to take some more stars and at the same time Francis took out an orb like device. He pressed a button on it and a force field appeared and covered the entire staircase and just then a few more stars from Norbert came but they bounced off the shield and lay on the ground.

'Come on move!' cried Francis and moved forward carrying the orb and so the shield also moved forward and shielded them from another ninja star attack.

Norbert saw this and then suddenly an idea entered his head and as they moved up another staircase, Norbert threw another star but instead of aiming for the shield he aimed it at the railing and the ninja star bounced off it and hit the wall and bounced off again and then hit the orb like device and cut through it! It fell down to the floor along with the cut in half device. With the orb gone so did the shield disappear as well.

Nick cried out 'How is that possible?! How could a wooden ninja star cut through metal?'

Norbert answered, 'This is no ordinary wood. This is special wood which can cut through any metal'. Then he took out another star and threw it at them and for the next two staircases Nick and Francis had no option except to dodge them.

As they emerged onto the third staircase they heard Snow announce, 'This is the last staircase to the top and afterwards just another staircase will lead us to the roof'.

'But Snow, how can this be the last staircase if there is one more to climb?' asked Flame.

Snow shook his head and muttered, 'How do I explain to him?'

Norbert suddenly took out two more ninja stars and threw them at Nick and Francis's feet. He threw them so fast that Nick and Francis had no time to dodge and the stars dug into their feet and knocked them off balance and they both fell onto the staircase.

The three cats had reached the top and there was one more winding staircase up ahead which led to the roof and they ran up it. Nick and Francis dug out their ninja stars and tossed them aside and then charged upwards ignoring the pain in their legs. They reached the top and started charging towards the other staircase and as reached near it they heard Norbert say, 'Okay Snow use your claws and open the door.'

They heard a cry of pain just as they reached and started running upwards and they heard Norbert say 'You two are the worst robbers ever!' and heard him pick the clock and heard it click open and the door opened as well. They suddenly came in sight of the cats as Norbert pushed open the door and Snow and Flame ran out and Norbert also ran out and tried to slam the door in their faces.

But just as the door was about to be slammed shut, at that moment, Nick jumped forward and pushed open the door and he and Francis ran out as the door shut. Their eyes darted around for the three cats and saw them climbing up a spire with some red sticky stuff on their paws and called out to them, 'Get down! Or we will blast you off!'

Norbert peeked his head at them and said, 'And damage the monument? I think not' and continued climbing and reached the top along with Snow and Flame.

Nick and Francis gritted their teeth but they knew he was right, 'They couldn't damage the monument just to catch some criminals' they thought.

Just then, there was an engine roar coming from somewhere nearby and a big red plane came out of the clouds. A door opened in its side and Night's head poked out from it and said, 'Jump! I will catch you!'

Flame and Snow cowardly jumped from the spire and came in touch with Night's paws and went inside the plane. Then Norbert smirked at Nick and Francis below and said, 'This time it is really see you never!' and jumped inside the plane.

Night shut the door and the plane which had been hovering near the spike took off into the dawn sky.

'Drat! Where is Simon? He should be here by now' cried out Nick in frustration.

Just then they heard Simon's voice coming from the side 'Guys over here now'.

They ran over and peered over the edge and saw Simon in their plane hovering close to the edge and then both jumped down into their seats. Simon said, 'Here we go!' and started moving the plane again in pursuit of the other plane and to hopefully catch the criminals.

But of course as you may have read earlier the plane which they had got from the Agency was an extremely slow plane and soon they were falling behind while Stryker's plane flew on ahead.

'We will never catch them at this rate!' cried Francis.

Nick said, 'I think it is time to use the two buttons we were told to only use in emergencies!' He pressed the blue button first and then a hatch opened on the back of the plane near the propellers and a black ball shot out and exploded into a haze of black of black smoke behind them.

'What the heck was that?' asked Simon.

'I think that is a smoke bomb which is supposed to distract the enemies while you escape' answered Francis.

'Well that doesn't help us when the enemy is in front of us and we need to catch them! Not distract them!' yelled Nick and he pressed the yellow button.

Two white pipes came out of the front of the plane and sprayed white smoke which covered them and the plane entirely and made them choke a little.

'What is this for?' cried Nick, his eyes watering.

'I think this is supposed to hide us from view from our enemy' said Francis in the same condition and then added 'Simon, hurry up and get us out of this'.

Simon nodded and piloted the plane in a few different directions and soon they were out of the smoke and in the sunshine again but their relief was short-lived as they looked ahead and saw Stryker's plane was about to reach the border in two-three minutes.

'Oh no! Once they cross the border we will lose them' yelled Francis.

'Well, there is only one option left' said Nick sighing and he opened the glass hatch containing the red button and prepared to press it.

But Simon said, 'Nick wait, they told us not to press it.'

'Well Simon, this is our only option left to catch them and let us hope this button produces a miracle' and saying that he pressed the button. Immediately the plane broke into different pieces and the three were separated and were left hanging onto the piece they were on.

Each was having a hard time. Nick was left hanging by his front paws on his piece and he couldn't climb up onto it because it was too small to take his entire weight.

Francis was standing near the centre of his piece but he could barely move around as the piece was very narrow and if he moved even a little bit his paw would skid and he would fall over the edge!

As for Simon his piece was the smallest and only one paw gripped it extremely tight while the rest of his body was in the air.

Just then, when all hope was lost for them the pieces started to come back to together but instead of forming into the plane shape they all formed a long straight shape with the front of the plane in front of the new shape and behind them, flames started to come out of the back and they shot forward faster and were quickly closing the distance between them and Stryker's plane.

Simon cried out 'I recognize this thing now, it is a rocket and it will blast Stryker's plane into smithereens but take us with it. How do we escape from this?'.

Nick quickly looked around and spotted the Seine River below them and cried, 'Quick! Jump into the river!'

They quickly grabbed their gadget bags and jumped down, the cats not even caring about their fur getting wet. They all landed with a big splash and when they all resurfaced, they saw the rocket was about to hit the plane.

Inside Stryker's plane meanwhile, the six cats along with Stryker were in the cockpit as the back room had been used for storing their stolen goods and the cockpit itself was not very big and only the plane controls were there.

'Yes! We stole the painting and successfully escaped from the trio and their tortoise plane!' cried Norbert and all the other cats and Stryker yelled triumphantly as well.

Night peered out of the plane to get some fresh air and he looked behind the plane and his smile disappeared.

He turned back inside and said, 'I think we have to cancel the victory party'.

'Why what's wrong?' asked Stryker.

Night answered, 'There is a rocket which is about to hit us in about three seconds' and as he finished saying this the rocket finally came in with the back of the plane and it exploded and completely destroyed the entire plane.

There was a lot of black smoke in the sky where the explosion had happened and the cats, along with Stryker, were sent flying in the sky completely blackened with Night being even more blackened than before.

They were flying up at a fast pace leaving a trail of smoke behind them and Stryker was flying in the same way as his wing was still dislocated and he couldn't fly properly.

'I actually thought we were gonna win this time' said Norbert.

Snow said, 'Boss don't you know that bad guys never win!'

Flame said, 'I have a question I want to ask, will we have bigger roles in the next adventure?' and they all flew off in the early morning sky and soon disappeared.

Down on the ground Nick and the others had climbed out of the river and had climbed up some stairs onto a street.

As they looked up to where some smoke still lingered from the explosion, they saw the stolen goods had miraculously survived with only being a little blackened and burned and were falling toward them.

'Quick we have to catch them!' cried Simon and they all caught the stolen goods as they fell close to them with their paws and placed them behind a bush next to them.

After half a minute Francis said, 'I think that is all of them!'

Nick looked up and said, 'Wait, there is still one more coming'.

The two cats looked up and saw the Mona Lisa falling which was the only one completely unscathed from the explosion was falling quickly towards the ground and Francis said, 'It's too big for one of us so we will have to catch it together'.

So they all gathered together and as it fell close to them they rose up with their paws and caught the edge together and stumbling a little managed to place it behind the bush.

'Phew! It's safe' said Nick and then he saw that some humans were coming towards the place where they all were and were definitely checking out everything.

Francis said, 'Quick! Let us run before they see us' and they all ran across a nearby bridge. They ducked down the nearest alley on the other side and stood catching their breath.

'I think the humans will definitely find those goods and return it to their rightful owners' said Simon.

Just then Nick jumped up and said, 'I just realized! We have failed our mission, we were supposed to catch the cats and Stryker but they got away Oh! What will we say to the High Council when we get back?'

'Speaking of getting back' said Simon. 'How are we going to do that now? When our plane is destroyed and there is no other transport that we have. I think we should stowaway on a goods ship headed to London.'

Then he turned to Nick and said, 'Don't feel bad they did not escape intentionally and at least they did not get away with their stolen goods'.

'Well I suppose you are right' said Nick.

Just then Francis said to Simon, 'There is still one thing that puzzles, me what did you tell the High Council mouse all the way at the beginning of the adventure to convince him for you to come with us?'

Simon smiled and said, 'Why I told him his name which the High Council generally keeps a secret.'

Nick asked, 'How did you know it and what is it?' Simon answered 'As I said before I am a know-it-all and I won't tell you two as it is a secret and enough of talking. Let us go to the dock and see if there are any goods ships headed to London'.

He ran off towards the coast with Nick and Francis running after him still bugging him about the name and Simon said quietly to himself, 'Don't worry Mike I won't tell anybody your name including these two'.

Epilogue

N orbert be careful with my wing please' requested Stryker as Norbert tried to put it back into the right position.

Norbert replied, 'Yes I will be' and he pushed the dislocated wing back into place.

Stryker cried out, 'Ouch!' and then said, 'Thank you Norbert I think I will sit here for some time'.

Norbert nodded and looked around him and we see that they arc in a small forest not far from Paris where they had crash landed into the branches of the trees which had broken their fall but given them some aching bones in return.

'Hey!' he called to the other five cats who were looking at a world map trying to figure out where to go into hiding. 'Have you come up with a decision yet?'

'Yes' answered Flame. 'We are going to Fiji.'

'Wait I thought we said we'd go to Hawaii' said Snow.

Night said, 'We agreed on Brazil'.

Leaf then said, 'I thought we voted for Congo'

Shorty said, 'No we are going to Russia'.

'Fiji!' said Flame.

'Hawaii!' said Snow.

'Brazil!' said Night.

'Congo!' said Leaf.

'Russia!' said Shorty.

'Fiji!'

'Hawaii!'

'Brazil!'

'Congo!'

'Russia!'

'Shut up!' said Norbert eager to put an end to the argument before it got out of hand. 'I am the leader and I say we go to Washington D.C.'

'Boss you can't decide this' said Snow and the others nodded.

Flame said, 'Let us all have a wrestling match together and whoever wins that cat's decision will be final' and the others including Norbert nodded.

Then they all leaped into a writhing mass of bodies wrestling against each other and nearby Stryker buried his face in one of his talons and muttered 'What idiots I should have never employed them!'

www.ingramcontent.com/pod-product-compliance
Lightning Source LLC
Chambersburg PA
CBHW072356020726
47506CB00004B/1143